KT-132-567

ARCHER'S LUCK

When drifter Lew Archer meets a priest while travelling along a lonely road in Texas, he thinks nothing of it. But this chance encounter sets in motion a train of events which sees Archer escorting a party of nuns through hostile territory to start a school on the Mexican border. With war and bloodshed around them, Lew Archer is the best man to help them make their way to safety, although why he should take the trouble to do so is a mystery to everybody — including Archer himself!

ED ROBERTS

ARCHER'S LUCK

Complete and Unabridged

LINFORD
Leicester

First published in Great Britain in 2017 by
Robert Hale
an imprint of The Crowood Press
Wiltshire

First Linford Edition
published 2019
by arrangement with
The Crowood Press
Wiltshire

A catalogue record for this book is available
from the British Library.

ISBN 978–1–4448–4345–3

Published by
F. A. Thorpe (Publishing)
Anstey, Leicestershire

Set by Words & Graphics Ltd.
Anstey, Leicestershire
Printed and bound in Great Britain by
T. J. International Ltd., Padstow, Cornwall

This book is printed on acid-free paper

1

There was a lot of nonsense talked in those days about so-called professional gamblers, but the fact was that there really were no such creatures. Those who made a living at play only managed to do so because they had an edge, which, in plain language, invariably meant that they were cheating. This in turn signified, of course, that when you heard that a man's livelihood was gambling, you could be pretty sure that he was nothing more than a cardsharp.

Such a one was Lew Archer, who, since his discharge from the Army at the end of the war, had drifted from town to town, trying his hand at all manner of things. Ranch-hand, rustler, scout, even lawman for a spell. After a while, Archer had settled down to running crooked poker games. You didn't tend to grow rich at this racket, unless you worked the big cities, but to do that you had to be very skilled indeed at cheating. Truth to tell, Archer wasn't all that good at what he did for a living. Still, he didn't need to be for his end of the market, which generally consisted of drunken cowboys and slow-witted sod-busters.

Lew Archer was working his way very slowly south, with no particular aim in mind, other than to rook enough men of their money to keep him in whiskey and ensure that he didn't have to get a proper job. He was not a greedy or ambitious man and as long as he had a few dollars in his pocket and the occasional girl on his arm, he was pretty well happy and contented. Lately, however, he had been feeling a mite dissatisfied with this way of life and beginning to think that there might be other and more honourable ways for a man to earn his daily bread. His travels and erratic lifestyle had, by the early fall of 1868, brought him down through Kansas and into Texas.

The routine which Archer followed

was a simple and well established one. He would fetch up in some small town, many of them little more than hamlets consisting only of a tavern and a dozen other buildings, and then sit playing solitaire by himself until some drinker asked him if he'd care to play a hand or two of cards, rather than sit there fooling around with the deck like a kid. He had never, since his career had begun, needed to invite others to play with him. It was always somebody else who first talked of a few hands of poker. This was a useful circumstance when, as was so often the case, accusations of cheating began flying around later. He was able to remind the sore loser that playing for money had been his own idea and that he, Lew Archer, had just been sitting by his own self, minding his business. There were usually witnesses, other drinkers who could affirm that this was the case and that Archer had not tried to inveigle anybody into a game of poker.

Mind, that was not always enough to

prevent unpleasantness and there were, from time to time, those who chose to take matters further and recover their money by main force. This was where professional gamblers needed the other skill which went hand in hand with cheating at play: the ability to be swifter and more accurate in the use of fists or firearms than those whom they had lately been fleecing of their cash. Men like Lew Archer had to be ready, willing and able to beat or kill a fellow being at the drop of a hat.

It was a fine September morning and the sky was that beautiful pale blue that you get down in those parts at that time of year. Archer had that morning left the scene of his latest conquest with the better part of $150 to his name and was now riding south-east, in the direction of another little town by the name of Indian Ridge. The night before, there had been some species of aggravation in the place where he had spent the last two days. The first night had been easy enough and he had cleared $260 playing with three farmers. Then the following night, things had turned ugly.

After a good win, it was his custom to stay on for a space in case any local men who prided themselves on their ability at poker might feel inclined to challenge him to a few hands in order to demonstrate their own prowess at cards to their neighbours and drinking partners. That was fine; it was all added profit. Last night, though, two of the men he had robbed blind the previous evening turned up with a fellow who Archer could see at once was going to be trouble. He was a hired hand on some farm and had a mean and crafty look about him. It was immediately obvious that this fellow fancied himself as a card player, and also that he was on to one or two of the most common methods of cheating.

All this was vexing, because it meant that Archer was obliged to play straight for once. This happened from time to time and was an irritation rather than any great hardship. He was a tolerable good player anyway, even without the sharping, and he could often win at poker by his skill at bluffing and calculating the odds alone. Still and all, sometimes the cards ran against him and that night, he found that he was down by the end of three hours play to the tune of $200 or so. That was fine too, because he was still sixty up; it just meant that his profits would be a little less than he had been expecting. It was at this point that the mean-looking man had accused him, unjustifiably, of cheating.

Now there is nothing more irksome than to find yourself charged with dishonesty when you have been making particular efforts to avoid anything underhand. Archer was a couple of hundred dollars down, due solely to this fellow's presence and that did nothing to sweeten his temper, either. He should perhaps have used his tongue a little more and his fists a little less, but he had been so infuriated at its being suggested that he was cheating, when he had just lost nearly $200 through being compelled to play straight, that he had given the man a methodical and scientific beating.

The atmosphere had changed after that and although nobody seemed inclined to challenge him further, it was clear that the suspicion lingered that he had been caught out at sharp practice and then attacked this man in a rage at being detected in the act of cheating. Archer had half expected to be jumped before leaving town that day so when he had chanced to glance back that morning and seen a lone rider apparently trailing him at a distance, but now gaining fast, his hackles rose and he thought at once that somebody was coming after him with a view to robbing and perhaps shooting him.

Now this is the difficulty with men of that brand who live by their wits and spend their days stealing from those they meet; it makes them constantly fearful that others around them are up to the same game. All Lew Archer saw that day was a bearded man on a pony coming up behind him at a smart trot, but it was more than enough to awaken in his mind the liveliest apprehensions of robbery, murder and the Lord knows what else.

The man was maybe a mile and a half behind, but gaining on him. There was a wood up ahead and Archer spurred his horse into a canter and then, as soon as he was out of sight of the man following him, ducked into the trees and prepared a little ambush of his own account. He drew the pistol which never left his hip during his waking hours and waited.

Through the branches and leaves, Archer saw the other rider enter the wood. He cocked the pistol with his thumb and then rode swiftly forward, crying as he did so, 'Stand to and throw down your weapon!'

The man he had thus confronted was perhaps in his late forties and dressed all in black. He also had a bushy black beard which cascaded down the front of his chest. When he caught sight of Archer and heard his challenge, he laughed out loud and said, 'I have no weapons to throw down, son.'

The younger man eyed the other with suspicion and asked, 'What's the game then? Why are you following me?'

'Why, because we seemed to be travelling the same road and I thought that we might ride along together. I was aiming to catch up with you, but then you bolted. Solitary travel can get mighty tiresome, you know.'

'I never found it so,' said Archer, still unsure of the other man's intentions. 'Truth to tell, I'm fond enough of my own company.'

'I'm sorry to hear it,' was the surprising response to this statement. 'A man who avoids his fellow men in that way is usually either very good or very bad. Are you a hermit or ascetic, something of that sort?'

'This is a blazing strange conversation to be having with a man I never set eyes on before in my life,' observed Lew Archer. 'Suppose you tell me who you are and where you're headed?'

The middle aged man smiled and shook his head sadly. 'You are that suspicious that I'll wager you get along by preying on your fellow men and women. I thought as much. No wonder you thought I was following you to do you harm. Like it says in scripture, 'The wicked flee where none pursueth'.'

'Wicked?' said Archer, vastly affronted. 'I ain't wicked.' He realized that he was still aiming his cocked pistol towards this fellow, who was at worst a harmless lunatic, and that this did not really lend any strength to his claim not to be wicked. He lowered the hammer carefully with his thumb and replaced the weapon in its holster. As he did so, the other rider turned his head slightly, affording Archer a brief view of the man's throat, around which was a white, clerical collar. 'You a preacher?' he asked.

'Jesuit,' corrected the man amiably, 'I'm a priest heading south to Sonara.'

Still not sure of the fellow, although relieved to find that he was not an enemy, seeking to shed his blood,

Archer said, 'You're off your track then. This here road leads to Indian Ridge. If you're heading for Sonora, then you coulda took the road south back aways.'

'What a suspicious mind you have,' said the priest sorrowfully. 'As it happens, I have business to conduct first in Indian Ridge, before I go to Sonora. Listen, my friend, since you prefer to travel alone, why don't we part company now and go our separate ways? I'm sorry to have alarmed you.'

Lew Archer had been thinking and he did not reply for a moment. Then he said, 'No, I reckon I'll ride along of you for a spell, Father. You don't want to be on the trail alone here. There are a lot of bad men about. I'll go with you to Indian Ridge. Mind, though, it will mean us camping out together tonight. But if you don't mind my company, I don't mind yours.'

It was said ungraciously enough, but Archer was horrified at the idea of a man of God travelling alone down this hazardous road.

11

The priest smiled warmly at him after hearing this gruff invitation. 'I'm not afeared of aught I might find on the road,' he said, 'but your concern does you credit, my boy. Come, the day's wearing away. Let's be on our way now or we'll not hit Indian Ridge this side of Thanksgiving.'

'Well,' said Archer, not entirely pleased at having saddled himself with an unwanted travelling companion, 'my name's Archer, Lew Archer.'

The other man rode forward and stretched out his hand. 'Father Joseph. And I am very pleased to make your acquaintance, Mr Archer.'

After they had been on the road for maybe five minutes, Father Joseph said, 'Why did you not like the idea of leaving a priest to ride this road by his self, Mr Archer?'

'You don't know about the trouble with the Kiowa and Comanche?' said Archer in surprise. 'It's practically open war hereabouts 'tween them and the bluecoats.'

'I know all that well enough. I was wondering why it bothered you to think of a priest falling into danger. You don't mind my saying, you strike me as a man who cares for little other than his own safety and wellbeing.'

Archer laughed at that. 'Maybe you're right at that,' he admitted. 'Mind, a priest is another thing.'

'You're Catholic?'

'I was,' said Archer shortly and the tone of his voice invited no further discussion of the topic.

'Come, Mr Archer,' said the priest, after they had travelled in silence for another ten minutes, 'won't you tell me a little about yourself? In return, I'll give you the outline of my own history.'

'Ain't overly interested to hear about it, begging your pardon, Father. As for me, I left the army three years ago when I was twenty. I'd learned to shoot and kill, I was good with cards and so here I am.'

'You make your money from cards, is that it?'

'That's it.'

'Well then, I entered a seminary back East when I was only eighteen. That was thirty years ago and I have been a priest for most of that time. Now I'm going to Sonora to take some money to the convent there. They have it in mind to start a school down that way.'

Archer turned sharply, a look of concern in his eyes. 'You're carrying money? How much?'

'Three thousand dollars. Why, you're not planning to rob me?' There was a twinkle in his eyes as he said this, as much as to say, 'Only kidding, son, I know that you wouldn't really do such a thing.'

'I don't know what you're thinking of, Father. I might not rob you, but an unarmed man carrying that much across this territory? I'll take oath that somebody will get that money before you reach Sonora.'

Father Joseph looked at Archer with a strange and unfathomable expression on his face. Then he nodded and said, half to himself, 'I was sure you couldn't be too far down the path of wickedness and now I have it confirmed. What a mercy that I met you.'

'That's nothing to the purpose,' said Archer roughly. 'The question is, what's to be done? You can't wander around like this with all that money. Couldn't you have had it wired to Sonora or something? Why are you carrying it like this?'

'It's a long story.'

At length, Archer said, 'I will stay with you to Indian Ridge and then we will think further on this.'

'Why should you care what happens to me?' asked the priest, apparently in amusement. 'I thought you prided yourself on being a man who only took care of his own interests. Isn't that how you represent yourself to the world? There's more to the case tucked away in your soul than people know of.'

'Never you mind about my soul,' said the other man, with a flash of anger. 'That's you damned priests all over, always meddling with other men's souls and such like. My soul is my own affair, not yours.'

Father Joseph said nothing more and they rode on together. At about midday, they stopped for a bite to eat. The priest was a skinny man and evidently in the habit of eating little. Archer offered him a share of what he was carrying, but Father Joseph declined, intimating that he was on some penance which entailed a restricted diet. This irritated Archer and he said, 'You think your god cares what you eat?'

The priest looked up quickly and said, 'You're interested in what the Lord requires of a man? That's a beginning.'

'I was raised by you people,' said Archer unexpectedly, 'meaning Jesuits. It was in an orphan's asylum they run, away over West. I tell you now, those men were the biggest set of bastards that I ever come across and I have seen some bad men in my time.'

If he had expected the priest to be

16

shocked or indignant about this statement, then he was mistaken, because Father Joseph merely shook his head and sighed. 'Yes,' he said, 'There are bad priests as well as good. They were cruel to you, no doubt?'

'You might say so.'

'Tell me now, did you ever meet a bad saloon keeper?'

'I reckon I've met such, yes,' said Archer.

'You think that they are all bad types?'

Archer considered the question, before saying, 'No, I wouldn't say so. There are good and bad.'

'It's the self-same thing with priests,' said Father Joseph, 'there's good and bad in all lines of work. A bad priest can be the very devil. Believe me, I know.'

They camped that night by a little stream which ran down from some rocky hills. There was a cluster of boulders which made a convenient and sheltered spot. Archer had not felt much like talking further of his life and had allowed the priest to talk about the things he had seen and places he had visited in recent years. They turned out to know some of the same towns and this made for pleasant enough, inconsequential talk, which suited Archer very well.

Before they turned in, Father Joseph invited the younger man to pray with him, a suggestion which Archer refused with more firmness than politeness. As he lay there in the darkness, he wondered what he should do about the man. He would certainly see him safe to Indian Ridge, but maybe he could find a way to set him on his way from there in the company of others. It surely made him uneasy to think of this decent man travelling around Texas just now with $3,000 in cash money about his person. He drifted off to sleep while turning this question over in his mind.

2

Not having to get up at any particular hour in the morning, on account of his work not starting until eight or nine in the evening as a general rule, meant that Lew Archer was in the habit of awaking slowly and in a very leisurely and unhurriedly fashion. On this morning though, he was jolted awake with a shock.

The unmistakable, sharp, metallic click of a gun being cocked near his ear catapulted him into consciousness in the merest fraction of a second. The gun in question, a Springfield breechloader, was held so close to his head that he could smell the oil on it. Archer was careful not to make any sudden movements such as might have been open to misinterpretation. He swivelled his eyes around and saw that Father Joseph was also being covered with a rifle. He too was awake. Before alerting the sleeping men to their presence, the two men who were now holding them at gunpoint had taken the trouble to remove Archer's gun belt from where it had lain beside the saddle-bag serving him as a pillow.

'What's to do?' asked Archer, although he knew the answer very well. These two rogues were road agents, like the old-time highwaymen that once robbed travellers in England. All they were after was money, gold or anything else worth stealing.

'Why,' said the fellow covering him, 'we'll just thank ye to hand over your money to begin with. 'Less you'd sooner we shot you first and then searched your body?'

'I'll pass on that hand,' said Archer. 'My wallet is tucked under my head. I needs must reach up for it.'

'Do that and you're a dead man. I'll take your bag now, while you just stay still.'

There was little enough to be done

under these circumstances and the best that he and the priest could hope was that they escaped with their lives. It wasn't unknown for characters like this to kill their victims after robbing them, just to do away with witnesses. They would have to hope that these men were not of that kind. Then he heard Father Joseph say in a firm, but pleasant, voice, 'I can't let you have the money I'm carrying. It's for children.'

The two men both laughed at this and then the one who was aiming his gun at Father Joseph said in an ugly voice, ''Can't' be damned to ye. Just move away from that pack of yours. Slowly now.'

Thinking the matter over later, Archer could never quite figure out what had gone wrong. Whether the priest had moved too quickly or perhaps because the man holding the rifle had cocked his piece and was already taking first pull on the trigger or maybe from some other cause, there was the sudden, sharp crack as the rifle went off. After that, things were pretty lively, at least for a second or two.

As soon as he heard the shot, the man drawing down on Archer with the Springfield glanced automatically to his left, to see what was happening. This looked to be the only opportunity he was likely to get and Lew Archer took immediate advantage of it. He kicked up at once, knocking the rifle aside and causing that too to fire. As he did so, he dived his hand into his right boot, which stood neatly by the side of his saddle-bag, drawing the little Derringer muff pistol which he kept tucked away there for emergencies such as this. Then he shot the man who had had the drop on him, straight through his left eye.

The Springfields were single shots and the man whose gun had first gone off was still evidently surprised at the turn that events had taken. As soon as he had shot his man, Archer leapt to his feet and snatched the fellow's pistol from his holster, grabbing it a second before the owner fell dead. Then he whirled around and fired twice at the other bandit, shooting him once in the trunk and then again through his head, just to make sure.

'Shit!' said Archer. 'Begging your pardon, Father, but that was a close call.'

The other man did not reply and for a moment, Archer feared that he had been shot. He glanced down and was reassured to see that Father Joseph had that same confident and unworried look on his face and his lips were curled slightly upwards as though in gentle amusement.

'Well, boy,' said the priest calmly, as though remarking on the weather, 'it was a close call for you, but I fear it's death for me.'

Archer looked more closely and saw a small hole in the man's blanket, singed at the edges as though somebody had fired almost point-blank at it.

'Ah shit, no!' he exclaimed mournfully and knelt down to see what the damage was.

Father Joseph said quietly, 'Hush your profanity now and listen. We don't have much time.'

'No, don't say so, Father. It will be fine. Let me have a look.' He lifted up the blanket and saw at once that the case was hopeless. Bright crimson blood was flowing freely from a wound in the priest's chest. From the vivid colour, Archer guessed that the bullet had penetrated a lung. He had seen such wounds in the war and knew that there was nothing to be done.

'Let me try to make you comfortable,' he said hopelessly.

This seemed to rouse the dying man and he said irritably, 'Stop your fussing now and attend to what I tell you. I want you to take the money from my pack and deliver it to the Convent of the Sacred Heart in Sonora.'

'It's all right, Father, you'll make that journey yet. Don't talk so.'

'Hush up and listen to me,' said the priest, 'there's no time for that foolishness. I'm done for. I didn't need the look on your face when you saw that wound to tell me that. It's nothing. Now listen carefully. You know Sonora?'

'I never been there, no.'

'It doesn't signify. The convent there is run by the Sisters of Mercy. Can you remember that?'

'Yes, but . . . '

'There's no time for buts,' said Father Joseph, his breathing growing shallower and more rapid, 'I'm failing fast. That bullet went through my lung and I'm bleeding like a stuck hog. Go to the Convent of the Sacred Heart and deliver that money. Tell them what happened. You'll do it?'

'Yes, of course.'

'Good man.'

The priest closed his eyes for a moment. His face was ghostly and ashen, that terrible paleness that has a touch of blue to it. It was plain as a pikestaff to Lew Archer that the man would not last more than another minute or so. He said, 'Do you want me to pray for you, Father?'

The priest seemingly had no more breath to speak, because he just smiled faintly and gave a slight nod. Archer had not the faintest idea what prayer might be appropriate for such an occasion and cast back into his childhood. In the end, he decided that a Hail Mary would do as well as anything. He said in a strong, clear voice, 'Hail Mary, full of grace, the Lord is with thee. Blessed art thou among women and blessed is the fruit of thy womb, Jesus. Holy Mary, mother of God, pray for us sinners now and at the hour of our death. Amen.'

When he looked up, he found that Father Joseph had stopped breathing.

A terrible rage at the pointless death of such an innocuous man gripped Archer. He jumped up and kicked at the face of one of the dead road agents, shouting, 'You stupid, cowson bastard! Why did you do it?' Then he realized that such conduct was hardly fitting in such close proximity to what was, in effect, a death-bed and he was a little ashamed of himself. He felt like weeping with anger and frustration at the senseless death, but pulled himself together and considered what was to be done next.

After glaring balefully at the two dead robbers, Archer came to the conclusion that he was damned if he was going to bother burying them. Father Joseph, though, was another matter. If he was going to go to Sonora, then he had best double back on his tracks and then head south. Turning up somewhere with a dead priest would only delay matters and could jeopardize the whole enterprise. It would only take one awkward person to accuse him of robbing the dead man and it would all turn into a regular circus. It struck Archer that the best solution would be to bury the man right here.

The soil was dry and loose, so it was more a question of scraping a deep depression, rather than digging a proper grave. Before depositing the corpse in this narrow trench, Archer took everything out of the dead man's pockets and stowed them in his own pack without examining them. He would take those too with the money to the convent. Perhaps they would know if the man had any family who they could send these few, meagre remnants to.

After he had placed the priest gently in the grave, Archer covered him with the loose, sandy earth and then carefully piled a cairn of rocks over the corpse, to protect it from scavengers. Then he took the dead man's Bible and read a few passages of scripture; it was the best that he was able to manage in the way of a funeral service.

The $3,000 was a mixture of bills and gold coins. Archer sorted through it and then packed it securely in his saddle-bag. As an afterthought, before leaving, he searched the bodies of the two robbers, but they proved to be down to their last few cents. Lord knows how they had been living. The only thing worth taking was one of the rifles that the two thieves had been carrying. If they'd had horses, then the Lord knew where they had tethered them. Father Joseph's mount, he untacked and turned loose.

As he headed back along the way that he had only lately travelled in the opposite direction, Lew Archer thought about the $3,000 and wondered what in the world it was that was stopping him from simply making off with the money. It was more than he had ever had at one time, in the whole course of his life and enough to set him up comfortably in a little place of his own. Nobody would ever know and he had cheated enough men out of their money to be reasonably sure that his conscience would not trouble him too much about the matter after a week or two. Perhaps it was no more than superstition, a promise made to a dying man. Whatever the explanation, Archer knew that he could not do otherwise than make his way to this wretched convent and hand over the cash to the nuns there. It was a damned nuisance, but there it was.

The track leading south went on

interminably, with little to vary the monotony of the landscape. It was not a part of the country where Archer had ever been and he had no idea at all when he was apt to strike the next town. All the way along, he was keeping a sharp eye out for any sign of Indians. The cavalry had been charged with responsibility for herding the Comanche and Kiowa onto reservations and they were proving none too willing to go. Their resistance was being aided by the Comancheros, traders who were often next door to bandits and who relied upon the Indians for their trade. They bartered firearms, alcohol and tobacco for ponies and hides.

It was a long day in the saddle and just as the sun was sinking and Archer had resigned himself to another night out in the open, he came into sight of a small town. The cluster of white painted buildings looked more Mexican than anything he had hitherto seen in these parts, although here and there were traditional clapboard houses as well. He guessed that he might be able to get something to eat and perhaps a bed for the night into the bargain.

Santa Pueblo was bigger than some of the towns that Archer had lately stayed in, although still little more than a large village. There was a saloon, blacksmith, church and so on. It would do as a way-halt for the night. His first stop was the blacksmith's forge, where the ringing of a hammer told him that somebody was still at work, despite the lateness of the hour. He dismounted and stood at the door to the forge, waiting patiently for the man to finish hammering the ploughshare upon which he was working. When the smith saw Archer standing there, he stopped work and came over to ask what he was wanting.

'Well now,' said Archer, 'I could do with a mattress for the night and also somewhere for my horse to stay.'

'What's your business here?' asked the blacksmith cautiously.

'No more than finding a place to sleep and maybe a meal.'

'You're not after causing trouble? On the scout, maybe?'

'You're not the law?' asked Archer, irritably.

'Not a bit of it,' replied the other.

'Well then, my business is my own and nobody else's. If you don't know of somewhere I can sleep then say so. I don't take to a lot of foolish questions.'

The man didn't seem in the least put out or offended by hearing this, but said equably, 'I was asking because if you aren't up to anything, then my sister lets a room from time to time. I wouldn't send anybody to her who I didn't like the look of, though.'

Archer grunted and said apologetically, 'I've had a trying day. Truly, I am just heading south to Sonora and want to rest up. There's no more to it than that. I'm not a Comanchero or anything of that sort, if that's what worries you.'

The fellow stared hard at Archer for a second, before nodding his head and saying, 'I'll walk over there with you directly when I finish this.'

'Let me give you a hand there.'

'Well, that's right good of you. Can you work the bellows?'

The two men worked in silence and the job was soon done. As he took off his leather apron, the blacksmith said, 'You work in a forge before?'

'Kind of. I was in the Kentucky Horse for three years. During the war, you know.'

From what he could see of it, the town looked quiet enough to Archer as he and the smith strolled over to a little white painted house surrounded by a neat garden. He was introduced to Mrs Cartwright, an elderly widow with a spare room. After they had been introduced, she asked, 'What do you do, Mr Archer?' He looked puzzled and she elaborated, 'I mean, what sort of job have you?'

'I don't have a job, ma'am.'

'Oh, you're looking for work, is that it?'

'Not exactly,' Archer said and the

widow Cartwright gave him an odd look.

She gave him some cold ham for supper, accompanied by a couple of fried eggs. He didn't realize until he was setting at the table just how hungry he was. After he had eaten, he went out into the garden to smoke his pipe. When he went back into the house, he said, 'I have a mind to take a walk before I turn in for the night. You won't be locking up yet a whiles, I dare say?'

'No, not for an hour or two yet. I dare say your walk will take you to the saloon, which you will find if you turn left after walking out of my front gate.' Mrs Cartwright did not sound censorious when she said this, more like a woman who knows well enough where men's minds are tending when they express the desire to go for a walk before turning in for the night.

The saloon was a cramped and dingy little building, which put Archer in mind of a Mexican cantina. He only wanted the one drink before sleeping and did not intend to stay long. There was a group of men around the bar, all of whom seemed to know each other and every one of whom appeared to be three parts drunk. Archer threaded his way through the men with the utmost care, knowing how easily such gatherings could erupt into violence at something as trifling as a spilled drink. He was not quite careful enough, because one of the men, who was swaying all over the place, stumbled against Archer.

'You clumsy bastard,' the man said aggressively, 'why don't you look where you're going?'

Now Archer's immediate instinct was to set out the case plainly to this drunken fool and then see how much further he wished to take the matter. He was on the point of returning a sharp answer which would probably have resulted at the very least in a fist fight, when he suddenly recalled Father Joseph's money that he had sworn to deliver to the convent in Sonora. What if he got into a brawl or gunfight here and was unable to fulfil his mission? Not only would he be breaking faith with a dying man, but a heap of children would not afterwards get a chance to attend school. He accordingly bit his tongue and by an enormous effort, restrained himself, observing mildly to the drunk, 'Sorry about that. I wasn't looking where I was going. The fault was mine.'

There is a certain kind of bully who takes politeness for weakness and regards common courtesy as the sign of the inveterate coward. The fellow who had bumped into Lew Archer was seemingly one of this type, because Archer's apology did not satisfy him at all. Indeed, he appeared to treat it as an affront.

'The fault was yours? Yes, I should just about say it was, you son of a bitch. Wandering around like some damned cow in a barn. I ought to give you a slap.'

Never before in his life had Lew Archer allowed anybody to speak to him in such an insulting manner. Had it not been that he had a greater purpose, in the fulfilment of what he conceived to be an oath, then he would have thrashed this swaggering bully within an inch of his life. As it was, he simply turned on his heel and left the smoky room, walking back out into the fresh air. He more than half expected the man to follow him out and continue the quarrel, but this didn't happen.

Archer was trembling with suppressed fury as he walked back to Mrs Cartwright's house. He had the obscure feeling that he had been somehow buffaloed into a course of action which didn't suit him one little bit, that he was being forced to behave in thoroughly uncharacteristic ways. This only added to his rage and the sensation that he was being shoved around. But who it was that was pushing him in this way and compelling him to act against what he had always seen as his own nature, he was quite unable to say.

Mrs Cartwright was pleasantly surprised to see the young man return so soon. She felt that maybe she had misjudged him and that his intention all along really was no more than to take a short stroll up and down the road before bedtime. It was heartening to her to discover that not all young men these days were drunkards and gamblers. After exchanging a few words with her, her guest went up to his room at a decent, Godly hour, which behaviour also earned him credit in her eyes.

The next day, Lew Archer set off on the road to Sonora. He rose early and found Mrs Cartwright preparing him a substantial breakfast. He said, 'You have been right hospitable to me, ma'am. I appreciate it. Perhaps you would tell me how much I owe?'

She named a sum which would scarcely cover the cost of the food which he had consumed.

In the usual way of things, Archer had a sharp eye for a bargain and would argue down anybody who he was paying for a service; finding 101 reasons not to settle for the full amount that was being asked of him. On this occasion, though, he felt the opposite impulse and flatly refused to pay only what he was being asked. At first, he offered double the amount, but the widow Cartwright would not hear of it. After a little good natured wrangling, she finally agreed to accept half as much again as she had first asked for. After he had counted out the money for her, she gave him a strange look.

'What's wrong, ma'am?' asked Archer anxiously. 'Is one of them coins bad or something?'

'Nothing of the sort,' she said, laughing, 'it is just that you are the queerest fish to fetch up on these shores in a good, long space. I never had a paying guest argue with me that I am not charging him enough. It is a real novelty.'

'I like to pay my way.'

'Is that what it is, Mr Archer? You struck me when first I met you as a man of the other brand entirely. Meaning the sort of fellow who would avoid paying his way if ever he could manage it. No offence meant, I'm sure.'

Archer laughed out loud at this. 'None taken, ma'am. You're a good judge of men. Yes, that's the type I am and no mistake. Happen I'm getting old or going soft or some such.'

She looked at him steadily for a few seconds and then said, 'No, there's more to the case than that. Good luck, Mr Archer, in whatever venture you are about.'

After collecting his horse from the corral at the back of the blacksmith's, Lew Archer shook the dust of that place from his feet and made off south.

The ride to Sonora was uneventful in the main. Archer had a sixth sense which alerted him to danger and he always seemed to know when it was time to leave the beaten track and make himself scarce.

The whole of Texas seemed to him to be in turmoil. Apart from the fighting between General Sheridan's forces and the Kiowa, there was a whole heap of stuff brewing down on the border with

40

Mexico. A year earlier, the Mexicans had shot their president and somehow thrown the French army out of their country. This had not led to peace, from what Archer could make out, and many poor people were trying to seek refuge north into the United States. The US Army was busily engaged in trying to stop them from doing any such thing.

It was at times of war such as this that men often felt like gambling at cards for high stakes. It had been the same during the War Between the States. Men who thought that they might be killed in the near future often became reckless with their money. After all, what would it matter to them if they hazarded all their wealth on the turn of a card; they might not even be there the next day to worry about being poverty stricken.

This also irritated Lew Archer, because he knew that there were rich pickings to be had here, right this minute, for a man who was deft and handy with a deck of cards. Instead of which, he was racing through the territory on a fool's errand, giving up a larger cache of cash money than he had ever held before in his life. He must be mad!

3

The Convent of the Sacred Heart was an imposing, stuccoed building on the edge of town. It was a gloomy looking place as far as Archer was concerned, putting him in mind of an orphan's asylum or penitentiary. Tall railings surrounded the ground; whether to keep thieves out or the inmates in, he couldn't decide. The only entrance appeared to be a six foot high, wrought iron gate, which was locked. Archer shook it a few times and then noticed a bell-pull on one of the stone pillars at the side. He gave this a vigorous yank and waited.

A nun glided from the main building and approached the gate noiselessly. 'May I help you?' she asked in a voice which was as soft as it could have been without actually being a whisper.

'I need to see whoever's in charge

43

here,' said Archer, adding at the last moment, 'if you please, Sister.' His childhood reverence for those in holy orders was impossible to overcome and this too annoyed him. He just wanted to dump the money entrusted to him and get back to his ordinary life.

'I can take a message for you, sir.'

'I don't want to send a message,' said Archer irritably, 'I coulda done that by mail, if that was my intention. I need to see somebody.'

'We don't admit visitors,' said the little nun, as if that explained everything.

'Take a message then to your leader, the Reverend Mother. Tell her that I have seen a fellow called Father Joseph and I must talk to somebody here on what has chanced. I'll wait.'

The nun nodded and then drifted away again, as though she were moving not by means of feet but rather by very well oiled castors or something of that sort.

By the time that the nun returned,

Lew Archer was feeling mightily ticked off about the whole affair. He had wasted his time on this snipe hunt for long enough and here he was, being made to wait like a beggar at the gate. Just when he was half thinking that he might just dump the money through the railings and be damned to the whole thing, the nun came back and unlocked the gate. She invited Archer in and then carefully locked the gate again behind her. It gave him an uneasy feeling, knowing that he was now effectively trapped in this place.

He was led into the building and along a dark corridor which smelled of beeswax polish. They halted at a varnished oak door, at which the nun rapped quietly. A voice within said, 'Enter' and Archer was admitted to the study of what he took to be the head of the convent.

The woman sitting behind the desk could have been any age from thirty to sixty. Her face was smooth and unlined and there were none of the usual clues which one had about a woman's age; hair style, clothing and so on.

The nun who had led him here seemed to have crept off without saying farewell so he was left alone with this other woman. She indicated a chair and Archer sat down. He said, 'I met a man called Father Joseph on the road. He asked me to deliver some money to your convent. Here it is.' He took out the bag of cash and laid it on the desk between them. The woman said nothing and he felt obliged to expand a little on the story, saying, 'He was killed by robbers. Said something about this money being for a school. Here's the rest of his belongings.'

'I did not catch your name, Mr . . . ?'

'Archer, Lew Archer.'

'I am Mother Veronica.'

'Say, are you English? You don't sound like an American.'

'That's right. I am English, although I have lived in this country for many years. Tell me how Father Joseph died, if you will.'

Archer found himself telling the whole story to this calm and wise looking woman. He left out no detail, but she showed neither shock nor surprise at what he had to say, nor did she ask anything about he himself. After he had finished, she sat for a full minute without speaking.

Then she said, 'We are very grateful to you, Mr Archer, for bringing us this money. I don't know what would have happened if we had not received it.'

'Starting a school, hey?'

'Something of the sort, yes. It is for the Mexican children who have crossed the border in search of safety. Many of them are Indians.'

'Religious school, I suppose? Making 'em pray for their food and such?' Archer could not restrain himself, remembering his own unhappy childhood.

Mother Veronica regarded him in silence and then said, 'No, not a religious school. Just somewhere for them to be able to eat and learn to read. We are a teaching order, not missionaries.'

'How will you send this cash to the border?' he asked curiously.

'I'm not going to send it at all. I shall take it myself. I am travelling there with the three sisters who will be setting up the school.'

Archer could scarcely believe his ears. 'Begging your pardon, ma'am, but maybe you don't know how things are situated right now outside of your convent. There is fighting with the Kiowa, skirmishes on the border with irregular forces from Mexico. Why, the whole of Texas is boiling over like an ant hill. Can't you send a man to take the money?'

'That would hardly help us to arrange for our sisters who are going to be running the school.'

'You mean,' said Archer in disbelief, 'you're fixing to set up this school of yours near the border? Why, that's just crazy. Who's going with you to take care of you, protect you and such?'

'As I said, I am going with the three sisters and we shall take this money with us. Thank you for your help, Mr

Archer.' She reached for a bell on the desk, presumably to summon a nun to show him out.

'Wait a minute,' said Archer, 'do you mean that just you four nuns are going alone down to the Rio Grande? How will you get there? There's no railroad or anything.'

'We have two ox carts. Two of us will ride in each. We need the carts for the books and other equipment.'

'Ma'am, Sister, I mean, it's not to be thought of. You won't get more than a couple of miles before some road agent or bunch of Comancheros catches ahold of you. There's not only your money, those men traffic women as well.' He saw that Mother Veronica had a slight smile upon her face and he said in relief, 'Ah, I get it. You're joshing with me. I thought for a minute there that you were serious.'

'But I am serious, Mr Archer. We have been waiting for this money and now that we have it, we shall leave the day after tomorrow.'

'You will be robbed, massacred, I don't know what all else. Who will take care of you?'

'The Lord will provide,' said the nun and Archer looked into her eyes, receiving the shock of his life.

One time, maybe a year ago, he had been playing straight, with no opportunity for cheating. By sheer chance, he had found himself with an unbeatable hand, a straight flush in diamonds, from the king down. It was the sort of hand card players dream of and Archer played it for all that it was worth. The other men dropped out until it was just him and one other guy. The betting went higher and higher, with Archer knowing that he was in an almost unassailable position.

Finally, the other fellow paid to see and Archer laid down his flush. He had looked up into his opponent's face and met that same look in his eyes as he now saw in Mother Veronica's. It was a simple and unshakable confidence in being the winner. On that last occasion, the man had laid down a royal flush in spades and Archer had been left penniless and with a whole heap of debts into the bargain.

That look of cast-iron assurance was utterly unmistakable and to see it in the eyes of the Reverend Mother of a convent gave Archer a strange feeling. Still, there it was; Mother Veronica was evidently holding a royal against whatever else the world might lay down and she was prepared to go the limit on her hand.

'If you're determined to do this mad thing, then at least let me go along of you, so that I can set a watch upon you and your sisters,' Archer heard himself saying slowly, before muttering, 'mind, it's a damned nuisance.'

The nun did not appear to be in the slightest degree surprised at this sudden offer. In point of fact, she looked as though she had been expecting him to say this all along, which was maddening. Nor did she start babbling her gratitude at being offered an escort.

Instead, she said, 'Why would you do that, Mr Archer? I rather formed the impression that you felt some grudge against religious education. Why are you offering to help us in setting up our school?'

'That's nothing to the purpose,' said Archer brusquely. 'You need a guard and I am willing to undertake that office.'

For the first time since he had been ushered into the room, Mother Veronica smiled fully, her face illuminated with pleasure. She said, 'There now, Mr Archer, did I not say that the Lord would provide?'

'The Lord has no part of this,' said Archer. 'To be blunt with you, me and the Lord have not been on good terms for some years. I shouldn't think that he would choose me to be his servant at this late date.'

'We will be leaving the day after tomorrow. Do you have somewhere to stay until then?'

'There's no shortage of boarding

houses and hotels round this town. I will be fine.' He stood up to leave.

'Will you take some money to pay for your hotel?' said the Reverend Mother. 'If you are working for us, then it is only right that we should defray your expenses.'

'I ain't working for you, Sister,' said Archer emphatically. 'I have not worked for anybody, man nor woman, for some good long while. I will pay my own way.'

Mother Veronica rang the bell on her desk and the nun who had first shown him into the room appeared silently. She even managed to open the door without the least sound, not even the click of the handle as she turned it. Before leaving the room, Archer said to the seated nun, 'I will be here at nine in the morning, day after tomorrow. Do you want me to arrange for your provisions or anything?'

'Thank you, you are very kind, but that is all in hand. We shall be pleased to see you. By the way,' she said, pointing to the cash that Archer had laid down on the table, 'if you are going with us, you may as well be our banker. Perhaps you would like to take the money and continue to hold it for us?'

As he was escorted back to the entrance of the convent, Archer asked the little nun, 'Are you one of those going to start this school or whatever it is?'

'I am, yes.'

'Well then, I suppose that we had best introduce ourselves. I am Lew Archer and I will be going along with you and your friends.'

'I am Sister Theresa. You are to be our scout?'

'Something of the sort,' said Archer.

However he ran the question over in his mind, Archer could not quite find the right answer. His calculations always seemed to be out.

True, he had been heading south when he bumped into that damned priest, but this wasn't business. He would hardly have a chance to make any money on this little expedition. He felt again that odd sense of being railroaded into doing things against his own wishes, but that was all foolishness. He had volunteered himself for this trip and had only himself to blame for doing so. Still and all, he thought, as he strolled along the busy street, he could hardly have done otherwise. What sort of dog would let a bunch of nuns journey through that dangerous territory alone?

Archer asked in the first saloon he came to whether they rented rooms by the night. They did and he paid then and there for two nights. His horse would be well enough at the livery stable until he left town and so there was little for him to do but amuse himself as best he could for a day or two. After stowing his things in the room, he went down to the bar room and ordered a whiskey.

It was just after midday and the bar was pretty empty. There were only a half dozen men there, two of whom

Archer marked as being on the point of giving trouble, either to themselves or those around them. They had evidently been squabbling and there was a feeling in the air that the quarrel might erupt again at any moment. Both men were heeled, which meant that when they tried conclusions with each other, it could easily result in bloodshed or even death.

He had barely finished his whiskey, when Archer saw that things were about to turn very ugly. He had not been listening to what was being said by the two men standing side by side at the bar, but one of them said, 'You say that again, you whore's son, and I swear to God I'll kill you.'

'I'd like to see you try,' replied the other calmly.

'You would, would you? Well, ain't it your lucky day? Step a clear of the bar there and we'll see what happens.'

The barkeep said, 'Come on, boys, let's be friends. There's no call for this carry-on.' Both men ignored him.

Anybody will tell you that when two drunken men are determined to fight a duel like this, then anybody with the sense that God gave a goat will take great care to keep out of the way. Lew Archer knew this as well as any and better than most. Nevertheless, he felt an inexplicable and powerful urge to prevent what looked certain to be at least one death. The two men were facing each other warily and backing slowly away. One of them was walking backwards towards Archer and he was keenly aware that if the other man fired and missed, then he, Archer, would very likely stop the bullet.

As the man moving in his direction was almost upon him, Archer reached out his hand and placed it on the fellow's shoulder. Without taking his eyes from the man with whom he was proposing to exchange fire, the man said, 'Take your hand from me or I'll kill you as well.' Archer took his hand from the man's shoulder and then stepped away from the bar.

The other men present had moved well clear of the two men who were so intent on violence and even the barkeep had vanished, crouching behind the bar where he would be unlikely to catch any stray bullets. Archer walked forward and then deliberately stepped between the two men. They were about twenty feet apart and just about ready to draw. Not only was it a grave breach of etiquette to interfere in an affair like this, it was practically inviting one or both of the participants to drill him where he stood.

'You fellows don't want to be killing each other, I reckon,' said Archer quietly. 'Why not forget all this and have a drink with me? I'm paying.'

For a few tense seconds, life and death, his own life and death included, hung in the balance and Lew Archer knew with great clarity that these might be the last moments of his entire life. But then the tension began to ebb away and one of the men who had been so keen on killing his drinking companion, gave a short laugh, which sounded like the barking of an angry dog. He said to Archer, 'You surely have balls, my friend. You surely do. I'll take that drink with you.'

Those who had been hoping to witness a gunfight at close quarters were disappointed, but the barkeep was so relieved at the way things had panned out that he produced a bottle of whiskey, handing it to Archer and saying, 'Here, it's on the house.'

The two men who had been on the verge of fighting were too drunk to wonder about Archer's sudden and unexpected intervention in their quarrel, but a couple of the other drinkers eyed him with curiosity. It was not every day that you saw a man try, and fail, to commit suicide so publicly.

After a glass or two with the men whose fight he had prevented, Archer left the saloon and walked about a little. It was far from being the first time that he had come close to death in consequence of a bar room dispute, but it was certainly the first occasion that he had pulled a stunt like that. As he walked down Main Street, he said to himself, 'Lew, my boy, there is something not right with you. Maybe you're going loco. What the hell did it matter to you if those drunken fools wished to kill each other?'

After looking in on his horse, it struck Archer that he had best arrange his own provisions. He didn't want to be relying upon whatever those nuns were bringing along and he doubted anyway whether powder and shot would be among the necessaries that the Sisters of Mercy would be packing into their ox carts. He hunted out a gunsmith and went in.

'May I help you, sir?' asked the clerk.

'Yes, do you have caps for a Navy Colt?'

'Surely, we do. Anything else?'

'Yes, four ounces of fine grained powder and do you stock cartridges for a Springfield?'

'What model?'

'It's one of them muskets, converted to breech loaders in 1865,' said Archer,

'Takes a .58 rimfire.'

'Yes, we have those. Will that be all?'

'I could do with some shells for a Derringer if you have them.'

After the goods were parcelled up and paid for, Archer thought it might be worth pumping the clerk for information. He said, 'I hear things are getting a mite lively down near the Mexican border.'

'You might say so,' said the clerk. 'We have the Army coming through here pretty regular, what with one thing or another. If it's not fighting the Indians, it's trouble down on the Rio Grande.'

'That's what I thought. Tell me, did I hear that some of those nuns from your convent are supposed to be heading down south soon?'

'That's more than I know. I don't have much truck with Catholics, to speak plainly. We're Presbyterians mostly, around here.'

After the incident in the bar room, Archer was minded to give it a wide berth. After putting the ammunition and powder in his room, he went for another long walk, up into the hills which surrounded Sonora. When he returned to the town, he found that a troop of cavalry had arrived and was being quartered nearby for the night. Surely one of the men would be able to give him useful information on the state of play in the south of the state.

Several times in recent days, Archer had found himself behaving in quite uncharacteristic ways and now he found the urge to do so coming upon him once more. In the normal course of his life, he acquired information in a casual and unobtrusive way, always taking care not to let folk know what he was really trying to find out. It was second nature with him not to be open about questions, but to approach any enquiries in a roundabout and circuitous manner. He at first proposed to go about things in his usual, devious way, but then it occurred to him that there was really no need to do so. He could simply ask in a straightforward fashion what he wished to know.

The cavalry had set up their tents a little way outside the town and Archer walked down there after he had eaten and spoke to the first man he found, a grizzled and tough looking trooper.

'Sorry to bother you, friend,' he said, 'but I am going south with a bunch of nuns in a day or two. They are starting a school down near the border. What's it like there right now?'

The man seemed flattered to have his views and opinions solicited like this and he gave Archer a clear and somewhat reassuring answer. 'We got the border itself quietened down pretty well. Now that the French have left and the new president is asserting his self, there are fewer folk crossing the river into our side. There's a bunch of poor devils, though, chiefly women and children, who have lost their homes in the fighting over in Mexico. They're living the Lord knows how on our side of the border. What will become of them, I don't know.'

'These nuns I've picked up with,' said Archer, 'they hope to start a school for the children. You think that would work?'

'Can't see why not. There's enough of our men around there to make it safe enough.'

All this was very encouraging and Archer was beginning to think that things were better than he had feared. However, the cavalryman went on, 'Getting there, though, now that's another case entirely. There's skirmishing going on all over between here and about ten miles from the border.'

'Skirmishing?' asked Archer. 'Skirmishing with who? Mexicans?'

'No, Comanche mainly and their damned friends, the Comancheros. Kiowa are in on the game as well. It's a regular war through most of that territory south of here. You will need to have a strong escort.'

Strong escort, thought Archer to himself as he walked back to the saloon where he was staying. If a cardsharp with a rifle and two pistols counts as a strong escort, then that's what those foolish nuns have all right.

4

On the morning of Thursday, 17 September, 1868, an observer stationed on the road leading south out of the Texas town of Sonora would have seen a curious little group moving slowly along the dusty track. There were two covered wagons, drawn by oxen, together with a single rider, mounted on a fine palomino. Seated at the front of each of the ox carts were two nuns in voluminous, black habits.

Archer could not make up his mind whether or not he was doing something useful and worthwhile, or if he was behaving like a damned fool and mixing himself up with a business that would only lead to trouble for all concerned. Before setting off, he had made one last attempt to dissuade the Reverend Mother from making this trip, but he may as well have spoken to the wind for all the notice she took of his carefully reasoned out objections. She had reminded him courteously that he was himself under no obligation to accompany them and let him know that they, that is to say, she and her three Sisters, would be making the journey regardless of anything said by anybody in the world. The Lord had commanded her to undertake this project and there was an end to it.

He had already met Sister Theresa and just prior to leaving, Mother Veronica had introduced him to Sister Mary and Sister Agatha. They were as quiet as mice, just like all the other nuns that he had seen about the convent and showed no inclination to engage in conversation with him. One of them looked to be a pretty little thing who could not have been more than eighteen or nineteen, but she was as shy and reserved as somebody's maiden aunt. Mother Veronica was no more chatty than the rest, but at least she would from time to time exchange a few words with him. It was clear to Archer that this journey was not going to be anything like a jaunt.

According to Archer's figuring, it would take them the best part of a fortnight to reach the border. He hadn't enquired into the Sisters' sleeping arrangements, but for his own part assumed that he would be sleeping out in the open for at least fourteen or fifteen nights. Presumably the nuns could hunker down in their wagons or something; he really had no idea.

It was a glorious morning with the brightest blue sky you ever saw in your life, although with just the hint of a chill in the air, as though autumn wanted to remind you that she was on her way. Still, thought Archer to himself, the sun is shining and with luck, the only hardship I'm going to encounter is the tedium of taking care of a bunch of helpless women. It was true that he had no prospect of making any money over the next week or two, but then again, his expenses would be negligible. He had brought some chow of his own and Mother Veronica had insisted that he should share in the nuns' meals. Looking to his own interest, if it was true that the Army was occupying the border area, then there would surely be many opportunities for a few hands of poker once they reached the vicinity of the Rio Grande. He had been a soldier himself for four years and knew just how bored men got under such conditions. Those boys guarding the river crossings would jump at the chance of a decent game of cards.

His mind engaged in casual thoughts of this kind, Archer did not at first hear the Reverend Mother calling to him. Calling was perhaps the wrong word to describe the efforts made by Mother Veronica to attract his attention. She certainly wasn't bawling or hollering or anything as vulgar as that. Rather, she was speaking loudly and raising her hand, hoping that she could catch his eye. He felt a little ashamed of himself for not paying heed to the nuns and retreating into his own thoughts like this. Archer rode up to the wagon.

'What can I do for you, ma'am?' he asked.

'I was wondering how many stops you thought we should make today. You have more experience of these matters than I.'

Archer was a little taken aback at the question. He said slowly, 'Why, if we are budgeting for it, taking two weeks to reach the border, then we can take no more than one stop each day and that only for a half hour or so. You travel by ox cart before?'

'I cannot recollect that I ever did,' said the Reverend Mother, with the ghost of a smile flickering around the corners of her mouth. 'It is a novel and not altogether pleasant experience.'

The horse had fell in naturally alongside the wagon and adapted itself to the same maddeningly slow, plodding pace of the ox pulling the cart.

'Thing is, ma'am,' said Archer, 'these beasts are mighty slow. If we make fifteen miles in a day, then I would say you'll be lucky. That's about what they hope to cover in wagon trains. Most of them are drawn by oxen too, you know.'

'The sisters are feeling a little unwell,' said Mother Veronica. 'The swaying motion and the bumping up and down. I was hoping that we could stop from time to time to let them recover a little. I fear that they will be sick otherwise.'

He was surprised to hear a woman, especially a nun, speaking so bluntly of folk throwing up, but even so he was remorseless.

'Begging your pardon, ma'am, but you'll recall that I advised against this journey from the first word I heard of it. I tell you now that the sooner we make it to the border, the more chance there is of us all staying alive. If you turn it into a Sunday School outing, with your Sisters stopping to walk about and pick flowers or I don't know what all else, then we are not going to make it.'

The nun stared at him gravely for a second and then said in an even lower voice than usual, so that he had to strain his ears to catch her words, 'Is the danger really that great? You are not just trying to make me turn back?'

'I wouldn't lie to you, Sister. I tell you straight that even as things stand, this is like to prove the death of us. Delay for anything unnecessary and you are making it nigh on a certainty.'

'Very well. We will do as you advise and limit ourselves to just one stop.'

The young man touched his hat brim and was about to ride on ahead a space, when the nun spoke again. She said, 'I am very grateful to you for offering to come with us, Mr Archer. More grateful than you know. I make no doubt that the Lord will richly bless and reward you for it.'

Archer grinned at that. 'Well, ma'am, we shall see about that. Let's try and get ourselves safe across the next hundred miles before we start counting our blessings.'

That first day's travelling was a nightmare for the younger nuns. The

Reverend Mother seemed to adapt well enough to the jolting and swaying, or if she was suffering, she kept her own counsel about the matter. The three younger women, though, disappeared at intervals into the wagons where, Archer guessed, quite correctly, they vomited.

Riding a wagon on a rough track is not a pleasant experience for anybody. There is no suspension to speak of, not like a fine, horse drawn carriage and the consequence is that every bump or stone in the road will send passengers jerking upwards. This is particularly so because oxen are among the slowest of God's creatures, moving at the best of times with all the speed of an old man with asthma carrying a heavy sack up a steep hill. This sluggish pace magnifies all the bumps. When you are moving along briskly in a carriage, pulled by a lively horse, small imperfections in the surface over which you are being drawn are hardly noticed.

That evening, they stopped at sundown by a little stream. Archer tactfully kept out of the way as the nuns made camp, giving them time to attend to their needs in privacy. He suspected that it was enough of a torment for those delicate and modest young creatures to have to rub shoulders on a journey with a rough young fellow like him. The less he was in evidence, the better he supposed they liked it. Mother Veronica insisted though that they all break bread together, which he was glad to do.

They lit a fire for warmth and light, but did not cook food. The diet of the nuns looked to be sparse and unappetizing and Archer wished he had thought to bring a haunch of ham or something. There was enough bread, cheese and fruit to satisfy the appetite, but it was not really his idea of a hearty evening meal. The Reverend Mother had apparently observed that he knew the correct responses to the various prayers that she had intoned before eating, and during the meal she said, 'You are Catholic, Mr Archer?'

'Not overmuch,' he replied, 'I was raised by Jesuits. In an orphans' asylum, you know.'

'Ah, that would explain a good deal.'

'Would it?' said Archer coldly. 'Meaning that not all you religious types are cut from the same piece of cloth?'

'I dare say you have not been to church since you left that place.'

'You got that right,' said Archer, with great feeling. 'Them places plain give me the creeps. No offence meant, you understand, ma'am.'

That night, Archer went off about a quarter mile from the Sisters. Far enough to give them their privacy, but not so far that he could not be coming to their aid pretty swiftly if there was need. They were out in the wild now and no doubt about it. He gauged that they had covered about fifteen miles since leaving Sonora, and there were likely to be only a few scattered homesteads and hamlets now between them and the Army encampments on the north bank of the Rio Grande. The only other people living in this stretch of country were Indians, traders and of course the Comancheros.

The next day, he was up as soon as the sun was peeping over the hills to the east of them. He got up, stretched his legs a little and then walked down to where the wagons were parked. There was no sign of the nuns stirring yet, but he did not aim to let them lie there and start later in the day. The sooner they were on their way, the sooner that they would reach safety. Archer gave a warbling cry, like a red Indian brave in pursuit of his enemies. A frightened face peered out from one of the covered carts.

'Good morning, Sister,' he cried cheerfully to the girl, who he thought was Sister Agatha. 'Time to be moving. Can I rely on you to rouse your fellows? I'll be up on yonder ridge, while you get yourselves ready.'

The girl nodded without speaking.

There was nothing at all to be seen from the higher ground. The track that they were following stretched away into the distance, threading its way through the early morning mist. That meant nothing, of course. Violence and death generally arrived out of the blue, with no prior warning. There was no telling what lay ahead on the trail this day. Still, there was nothing to be seen for now. He went back to the wagons, where the younger nuns were looking as though they did not relish the prospect of another day's hard travelling. The Reverend Mother, though, was moving around with her back ramrod straight, issuing directions. She was a tough one, all right, thought Archer. She put him in mind of some tough old veteran, directing a bunch of raw recruits.

When she caught sight of him, Mother Veronica waved and he rode down to speak to her.

'Well, ma'am,' Archer said, 'it's not too late to turn back. It's still only a day's ride back to your convent.'

'Is that what you recommend, Mr Archer?'

'To speak plainly, it is.'

'Well then, I am sorry to disappoint you. We will be continuing on our way south. I suppose you wish us to start as soon as possible?'

'That's the strength of the case, yes, ma'am.'

They were on their way by 7.30, for which Archer was grateful. It was another fine day and the sunny morning was making him feel cheerful and optimistic. He was beginning to feel that things would go smoothly after all and that perhaps his presence had not been needed. That was until, a little before midday, he saw the cloud of dust in the distance which told him that a group of riders were heading towards them. He rode up at once to the wagon where Mother Veronica was struggling manfully to make the ox do as it was bid.

'It might be nothing, ma'am,' he said, 'but there are riders coming this way at a fair pace. I can't tell anything about them.' He said this in a low voice, hoping that she would understand his anxiety without the need to go into lengthy explanations.

'What do you suggest we do, Mr Archer?' asked Mother Veronica.

'Carry on as we are and then when they are a little closer, I will ride out to meet them.'

'Do you anticipate danger?'

'I don't know and that's the God's honest truth. It could be an Army patrol or Indians. Or bandits, for the matter of that. We must wait and see.'

They didn't have long to wait, because the riders were coming on at a fast trot and within ten minutes or so, Archer could see that it was a party of perhaps twenty or thirty men. If they were hostile, then it was all up for him and the Sisters. There seemed to be nothing for it but to ride straight out to meet them and see what was what. He told the Reverend Mother his intention and then set off at a canter. By then, he could see that the horseman were Indians and his heart sank. There all but open war at that time between the Indians and the Army, and the violence had spilled over into attacks on isolated farms and lone travellers. Right now, the Kiowa and Comanche were feeling none too well disposed towards white men and there was an excellent chance that the men he was riding out to meet would simply kill him on the spot.

As he grew closer to the riders, he could see that they were armed to the teeth and wearing war paint. Archer began to suspect that this encounter might be the death of him. He had faced death often enough during the war so the prospect was not as shocking to him as it might have been to an ordinary person. Even so, he was sorry to think about it. If they were in the mood for murder, then the best he could hope for was a clean death. He had in the past seen the remains of those who the Indians had tormented; devising lingering deaths for their victims that went on all day. Luckily, he had his pistol with him and at a pinch, he supposed that he would always be able to put a bullet in his own brain.

When the distance between him and the oncoming warriors was down to a hundred yards, Archer reined in and simply waited in the middle of the track. The Indians came on for another ninety yards or so and then they too stopped. It felt a pretty awkward sort of moment, with him holding the road against this entire war party. The Indians did not look to be in a hurry, but waited patiently for him to speak. Archer said in a loud voice, 'Any of you boys speak English?'

One of the men rode forward, a chief, by the look of him, with a splendid war bonnet made of eagles' feathers. He said, 'I speak English. Why are you here? Are you a soldier?'

'No,' said Archer, 'I ain't a soldier. I'm travelling with a group of nuns, God women. They want to teach some Mexican Indians to read and write. We're taking books south.'

'God women? You mean the black ladies?'

'Yes, they wear black all over.'

'These God women we know. They can pass. We do not make war on women or children. The black ladies help our people.'

So far, so good, thought Archer, but what about yours truly?

'You going to let me go as well?' he said. 'They need me to guide them and look after them. Will you let us all continue?'

One of the braves called out something to the man who seemed to be acting as the spokesman, who shouted something back angrily. Archer guessed that the first man had said the Indian equivalent of, 'Hurry up and stop wasting time on this idiot!' and that the chief had told him to shut up and keep quiet. The man who had rode forward to parlay with him said, 'You can go back to the God women and tell them they are safe from us. We go to fight the bluecoats. You may pass.'

'Thank you,' said Archer, feeling weak with relief.

Even when you've steeled yourself to face your own death, it is only human to be pleased when you learn that you will, after all, be living beyond that day. He saluted the Indians and then wheeled round and cantered back to the ox carts, before they changed their mind. He went straight to Mother Veronica and said, 'Whip up those oxen, ma'am. The Indians say that we can pass, but the sooner the better if I'm any judge of such things.'

Archer and the nuns moved forward and the Indians gave them the road, splitting into two columns and allowing the nuns to keep to the track. Other than that, they ignored the travellers. Once they were clear of the men, Archer said to the Reverend Mother, 'I reckon that was a narrow squeak. We might not be so lucky next time.'

The rest of the day was uneventful enough. They stopped by a stream at one point, to refill canteens and the wooden kegs in which the sisters stored their water. After snatching a morsel, they carried on without stopping until dusk.

After they had eaten their evening meal, Mother Veronica said to Archer, 'We could all do with some relaxation, Mr Archer. Can you entertain us perhaps? My sisters are finding this journey more trying than they expected and it would do all of us no harm to have our minds taken off things a little.'

'Well, ma'am,' said Archer apologetically, 'I don't know that I am the fellow to ask. I can't sing or recite or nothing like that. I don't play any instrument, either.' He thought for a bit and then said, 'We could play cards perhaps, for twigs or stones, I mean, not money.'

'Why, that's a grand idea.' The Reverend Mother turned to the young nuns and asked, 'Do any of you know how to play cards?' They all shook their heads shyly. 'Perhaps Mr Archer will undertake to teach us a game then?'

'The only game I really know is poker,' Archer said. 'I will engage to show you ladies the rules if you like.'

'There now,' said Mother Veronica, 'I knew that we could rely upon you to lift our spirits this evening. Do you have a pack of cards though, for us to play with?'

'I think I might have such a thing about me somewhere.'

And so began one of the oddest experiences of Lew Archer's life, sitting in the middle of wild country which was infested with hostile Indians and dangerous bandits, while he endeavoured to teach four nuns how to play five card draw poker.

5

If anybody had told Archer a week ago that he would soon be playing poker with nuns for twigs and stones, he would have laughed in that man's face. Still and all, here he was in just that very situation. He asked, 'Does anybody know anything at all about poker?'

To his surprise, the Reverend Mother said, 'I believe I recall seeing the game played many years ago. Before I took my vows, of course. Is it not the case that you must make up groups of cards in threes and fours or even pairs, and the person with the highest hand wins?'

'That's it, just right, Sister. Listen, why don't you and me play a hand or two and the other ladies can watch and learn?'

'Why, that sounds like a marvellous plan, Mr Archer. Will you deal, or shall I?'

'I must shuffle the deck first.'

86

After he had shuffled, Archer dealt the cards to him and the Reverend Mother, breaking them into two lots of twos and threes, rather than dealing five straight off. He laboriously explained the values of the various hands to the nuns and then demonstrated how to bet, while explaining such arcane terms as 'raising', 'holding' and 'folding'. To show how it was done, Archer dealt a few hands and then explained how he would have bet, which cards he would have held, which discarded and so on. Once he thought that Mother Veronica had the hang of it, he suggested that he and she played a hand and the sisters could watch and try to follow the play.

'Why don't you try shuffling?' he asked Mother Veronica. She did so and then, again at Archer's urging, she dealt the cards out.

Archer found himself with three kings, and two odd cards. This gave him the opportunity to show the women how 'raising' worked. He discarded two cards and the Reverend Mother took one. To his delight, he found that he had drawn a pair of queens to go with his kings. If only they had been playing for money, he thought sadly. And he hadn't even been rigging the deal. That was life all over: you get a great hand, by sheer chance, and then stand only to win a handful of pebbles for it! Still, a full house was a full house and so he raised Mother Veronica a couple of times until she paid to see him.

Archer laid down his cards proudly. The three younger nuns craned their heads forward to look and Mother Veronica said, 'Oh, isn't that what you called 'a full house' earlier?'

'That it is, ma'am and I'll warrant you have nothing to beat it.'

'I think that you said a full house beats two pairs?'

'That's right.'

'Well then,' she said, 'that's all that I have: two pairs of ones.'

'Two pairs of ones?' asked Archer, bewildered. 'I'm not sure that I take your meaning.'

The nun laid down her cards. What she had called 'two pairs of ones' were in reality nothing other than four aces.

'Well, I'm da . . . I mean, I am surprised,' said Archer. 'Sister, that hand of yours beats anything else in the world. You don't see four aces very often and that's a fact.'

Then a thought struck him. Hadn't one of his discards, the hand before, been an ace; the ace of hearts? How in the hell had that card ended up being dealt to Mother Veronica? He looked up, to see the nun smiling mischievously.

'I'm sorry, Mr Archer,' said Mother Veronica, 'I just couldn't help it. You looked so earnest and trusting, that temptation got the better of me. It was very wrong of me.'

'You mean,' said Archer, the realization slowly dawning, 'that you rigged that deal?'

'Of course,' she said briskly. 'Do you know the odds against drawing four aces?'

The young nuns were looking at their superior in amazement, wondering what she would say or do next. They were seeing a new side to the Reverend Mother on this trip.

'Sister, I've spent a lot of time gambling and I didn't spot what you were about. How d'you do it?'

'Just hid them in my sleeves, of course. These habits are surely big enough. Why, how would you have done it?'

'I'd a . . . '

There was a disconcerting gleam of triumph in Mother Veronica's eyes. 'Ah,' she said, 'So that's what you are. A cardsharp. Thank the Lord it's nothing worse. I couldn't make out what your line of business was, Mr Archer and now I know. It's a weight off my mind.'

'What d'ye mean, a weight off your mind?' asked Archer, thoroughly perplexed by now.

'I knew at once that you made your living by some means that you didn't want to share with me. I worried that you might be a hired killer or bank robber or all sorts of things. Now I see that you are only a thief. I am glad it's nothing worse.'

'Where did you learn to fool around with a deck of cards?' asked Archer, not caring for being called a thief.

'My brothers were a rare bunch of scoundrels. They were all older than me and they used to teach me all manner of tricks that no well brought up girl should know about. False shuffles and crooked deals were among the more harmless of their nonsense.'

The younger nuns then joined in and the evening passed pleasantly, but every so often Archer shot a glance at Mother Veronica. She had worked him just as he himself worked a mark, even down to letting the suggestion of a game of cards come from him. There was a good deal more about that nun than met the eye.

After he had moved away from the wagons to sleep, Archer found that his mind was oddly disturbed by the words which the Reverend Mother had spoken so casually. Incredible to relate, Lew Archer had never thought of himself as a thief. Indeed, he rather despised those who stole from ordinary people. He didn't mind a bank robber or somebody who took money from a big company, but he had always viewed men who stole from workers, farmers and other small types as being pretty low-down. And here was this nun casually telling him that she was glad he was no worse than a thief.

Before he fell asleep, Archer tried to reason the matter out in his mind. Was cheating at cards really stealing? Had he been a thief ever since he took up living by play? Being a professional gambler had an exciting flavour to it, made him sound like somebody. Even being called a cardsharp did not sound too bad. But being termed a thief, ridiculous as it might seem, that hurt.

The next day, they were on their way again at dawn. Archer thought that they were making pretty good time and that with luck, they would get to the border in less than a fortnight. The young nuns appeared to have got used to the motion of the ox carts, because they were not ducking into the back every few minutes now. They still did not talk much, at least not to Archer, but were definitely a little happier and more relaxed. He saw them smiling and chatting to each other as they rattled along. The atmosphere was, unless Archer was very much mistaken, more relaxed since the Reverend Mother had unbent and played her trick on him. It struck him that Mother Veronica's behaviour had made her somehow more human in the eyes of her charges.

Since Mother Veronica had called him a thief, Archer felt a little less apt to talk freely to her. That morning, he hardly rode alongside her wagon at all. She must have noticed this, because when they stopped to eat at midday, she came up and led him to one side.

'Are you annoyed with me, Mr Archer?' she asked frankly.

'I don't take to being called a thief, if

that's what you mean,' he told her.

'I never had you down for a coward, though,' she said. 'That does take me by surprise.'

'Coward?' exclaimed Archer, 'I ain't no coward. I was in the Army four years.'

'Somebody who shies away from the truth is a coward,' said Mother Veronica firmly, 'doesn't matter how many men you might kill in a battle. Refusing to face up to what you are is cowardice.'

Archer had had enough of this and simply walked off by himself, refusing to take any further part in the conversation.

An hour after they started on their way again after the midday break, their track went up a slight rise, so that they could not see what lay before them. When Archer came to the top of the slope, he could see that perhaps a mile ahead of them was another wagon. It was standing by the side of the road, with no sign of horses or any people around it. The sight of it raised his hackles and he knew that something was not right. He turned back and spoke to Mother Veronica.

'There's an unhitched wagon down the road a way. It looks pretty new to me, leastways, judging from the colour of the canvas hood. There's no horses near it, though. I'm afeared there's mischief afoot.'

'What kind of mischief?' asked Mother Veronica.

'Jiggered if I know. I would ride ahead and investigate, but that would mean leaving you and your girls here alone. I think we should all travel together towards it. But if I give the word, you all stop at once. Is that clear?'

'Just as you say, Mr Archer.'

He reached back into his saddle roll and pulled out the Springfield. Then, even though he knew he had loaded it himself, he double checked that there was a cartridge in the breech. After that, he cocked the piece and loosened the pistol at his hip, so that it would be sure to slip easily from the holster. The Reverend Mother watched these preparations and asked, 'Do you really think there is danger?'

'No harm in being ready.'

By the time that they reached the abandoned wagon, Archer was sure that there had been some villainy afoot. There were clothes and household goods scattered around the thing, making it look to him as though it had been conveying a family. He said to the nuns, 'Stop right there and don't move any further on.' Then he dismounted and went on to see what else was to be found. He soon wished that he had restrained his curiosity.

The first thing Archer did was peer into the wagon, just to make sure that there was nobody hidden inside who was likely to jump out and attack them. It was empty. The domestic goods dumped all over the ground had been the contents of the two wooden chests he could see. At a guess, this was a family of homesteaders on the trail.

There was no sign of life, though. He walked around the other side of the wagon and found a man of about thirty. He was stone dead and pinned to the side of the wagon by a long metal spike which had been driven through his throat. Near him lay a baby which could not have been more than six months old. It too was dead.

Archer had seen a whole heap of terrible things in the war, but nothing to match this. The savagery of men who would skewer somebody like that, as though he were no more than a hog, and then leave a baby to die, was unbelievable. He was determined that the nuns must not see this dreadful scene. When he turned, though, it was to find Mother Veronica standing behind him, surveying the wagon and the man nailed to it. He said, 'Come away from here, ma'am. This is not a fitting thing for you to see.'

'Nonsense. It's my work. Is he the only victim?'

Archer indicated the dead baby and

she stooped at once to make sure that life was wholly extinct. Then she stood and said, 'I should say that child has been dead for twenty-four hours or so. I suppose that the man too has been dead that long. Look at the blood, it has turned quite black.'

'Ain't you sickened by this?' asked Archer. 'How can you stand there talking like that about a baby that's been killed?'

'They're beyond our aid now. Tell me how you read this, Mr Archer. What do you think took place here?'

He went over to where the personal possessions and clothes were lying scattered on the ground and then bent over to root through them. Then he stood up and said, 'I would think that this was a man and a woman, with their baby. Homesteaders, I guess. They was ambushed and the man killed. I see no marks on the baby, so maybe they just left it to die of hunger and thirst.'

'Where do you think his wife is?'

'Sister, I don't think we should stand

here talking. We must get away from this spot just as fast as we can.'

'Why? Who do you think did this?'

'I don't know. All I know is, we don't want the same band to catch ahold of you and your girls.'

To Archer's horror, Mother Veronica went over to the dead man and began examining the spike which held him pinned to the wagon. She wiggled it a little and then started looking around on the ground.

'Sister, what are you doing?' said Archer.

'Working out what happened to this poor devil,' she replied coolly. 'See here, there are five more of these metal spikes lying here, along with a large hammer. I suppose they are some sort of agricultural implement. I think this man fought them, perhaps injured or killed some of the attackers. They have done this to punish him.'

'So?'

'It wasn't Indians. They are much more ingenious than this when it comes to torture and death. I think he was killed by white men.'

He lost patience at this point, saying, 'All right, Reverend Mother, I'll tell you what is probably happening and then you'll see the need to cut sticks and get out of here fast. I think that this is the work of Comancheros. They have taken the woman to sell on, either to Indians or to smuggle across the river into Mexico. There are brothels there that pay right good money for pretty young white women. Those nuns of yours are young enough that they would fetch a fair price. Are you satisfied now?'

'Do we have time to bury these people?'

'Don't even think it for a moment,' said Archer shortly.

'Well then, I shall at least say a prayer.'

'So long as it's a quick one. I tell you now, we are apt to share the fate of these folk if we don't make tracks pretty fast.'

Not unsurprisingly, the discovery of

the dead family cast a shadow over the rest of that day. Archer did not know what the Reverend Mother told the other nuns, but it was enough to dampen their spirits a little. They had been rather gay after the way that their superior had unwound the previous night; now they were back to being quiet and subdued.

At Archer's insistence, the midday halt was cut from half an hour to twenty minutes. All the time that the nuns were eating and attending to their personal needs, he was prowling around restlessly, the rifle cradled in his arms. When they made camp that night, he approached Mother Veronica and took her off out of earshot of the others.

'Sister, we need to think this over. That wagon has put what you might call a different complexion upon this trip.'

'You mean that we should turn back and return to Sonora? We have been through this before, Mr Archer.'

'Some body of men killed that man, took his wife and left their baby to die in the wilderness. You got any notion what sort of men would behave so? I have known some mighty rough types during the war, but not a one of them would have done anything so beastly.'

'Mr Archer, the Lord told me to bring my Sisters out on this road and tend to the helpless children for whom no provision has been made. Homeless children, without mothers and fathers to care for them, no schools to teach them. Do you think I will abandon those children now, just because I have seen evidence of the barbarity of a bunch of violent men?'

'All I'll say is that your Lord is gambling with your lives. You got to hope that he is as good at rigging the cards as you and me, because otherwise, we'll all end up either dead or worse, you hear what I tell you?'

'Yes, I hear you well enough,' said the nun calmly, as though Archer had been mentioning the chances of it raining the next day.

Sitting around the fire that evening,

there was no enthusiasm on anybody's part for high jinks or fooling around with card games. The other sisters clearly had picked up on the tension between him and the Reverend Mother and did not want to get involved. They whispered softly to each other and were content to leave Mother Veronica and him to do the talking. Archer stared moodily into the flames and then said suddenly, 'If you think I'm a thief, then how come you want to let me hold your money for you? You ain't afraid I'm a going to run off with that?'

'Oh no,' said the Reverend Mother, 'you're not at all a man like that. You're a special kind of thief. You only steal from men and then only when they are strangers. You'd never dream of stealing from a friend.'

This was such a neat and accurate summing up of the business, that Archer was lost for words. 'Seems to me,' he growled, 'as you know more about me than I do myself.'

Mother Veronica appeared to take

this statement seriously. She said, 'No, I wouldn't quite say that, Mr Archer. There's good and bad in us all. We're all sinners. You've just plumped for a very narrow and particular kind of sinning. I'm sure that you're a good man in all other respects.'

'That's as maybe,' he said, 'but I aim to get some sleep now. It is enough for me to tackle the job in hand, without worrying overmuch about sinning. If you're agreeable, I think that we should start even earlier in the morning and try to get as far from this area as we are able.'

Once he had withdrawn from the nuns and left them to their own devices, Archer sat out on the hillside, considering fairly what the Reverend Mother had said. She had of course hit the nail bang on the head. He was a man who stole from strangers, men who were unknown to him. Put like that, it sounded a shabby enough way of life. Maybe, he thought, there are other things that a fellow like me could turn my hand to. Only thing is, I surely do not like working for a boss and being told what to do. I'm not rightly sure that I could settle to that now.

The great advantage of sharping is that you can live your life on the move, without being tied down to any one special location. In fact, all things considered, you had best live like that if your occupation is cheating other men out of their money at poker. Stay too long in one town and somebody is certain-sure to catch you out and spot what you are about and that can be as good as a death sentence. Next to rustling cattle, cheating at cards was perhaps the most frowned upon activity in many parts of the country.

As he lay down to sleep, Archer was thinking about his life and trying to square the way he had always represented himself in his own mind with the person that Mother Veronica had held up to his view: a mean thief who took money from ordinary folk at any chance he could get. Gambler, he thought, as he drifted off. Thief is more like it. She's got the measure of me, that one, and no mistake.

6

Archer was bolted out of his slumbers by the sound of hysterical screams. Even before he opened his eyes, he knew that somebody was attacking the nuns. He was sleeping in his clothes and all that was needed was to pull on his boots and pick up his guns. He did so and then, as he was beginning to run down the hill to protect the women he was escorting, he slowed right down and listened carefully. Mingled with the screams was the sound of men's voices. They were not exactly shouting, more speaking loudly and roughly to each other. It sounded to Archer as though there was a pretty sizeable bunch of men down there and it was this which caused him to pause and rethink his actions. He had sworn to himself to let no harm befall those four women, but it would not help them if he was to get his self shot.

He crouched down, so as not to make a silhouette against the sky. It was a new moon, which meant that there was complete darkness. Whoever was raiding the camp had stirred up the fire to provide light and in the glow from the flames, Archer could see that there were at least a dozen men surrounding the two wagons. They had dragged out the nuns and were pulling everything from the wagons, presumably looking for anything valuable. The precious school-books which the Sisters were taking to start their school were cast onto the fire, which flared up to illuminate the scene more clearly. He felt a killing rage begin to take hold of him at the sight of this wanton destruction and the consequent shattering of the nuns' dreams of that school. The temptation to run down there right now and kill as many of those bastards as he could was nearly overpowering. Nearly, but not quite.

The only thing to set his mind to now was how to save the lives of those four women. Nothing else, not the school books, the money he was carrying, nor aught else mattered a damn. Archer crawled closer, until he was perhaps a hundred yards from the scene. To his horror, he saw that the nuns were practically naked and the men were making coarse jokes about their condition. With those girls so modest and shy and all. It was almost more than he could bear and he averted his own eyes so as not to be compelled to witness their shame.

If Archer was any judge of men, the next step would be rape and then maybe murder. However, none of the men looked to be about to ravish the women and instead seemed keener on searching the Sisters' belongings, in hope of finding something worth stealing. While he observed the unfolding drama, it occurred to Archer that he couldn't understand what was being said by those men. He listened more carefully and found that they were speaking heavily accented Spanish. He knew a little of the language, but could hardly make out one word in twenty of what those men were saying.

The nuns were having their hands tied behind their backs, after being given their clothes. Whatever was going on here, it did not look to involve rape or murder; at least not yet. Archer couldn't decide whether or not he should fetch his horse. He was reluctant to do so, because he could move a damned sight quicker on his own two feet. It depended on what these men had next in mind.

Once the women had had their wrists tied, one of the men linked them all together with a long rope. Then the men jumped onto their horses and set off at a walk, with the women being led on foot. In some ways, this was good, because it meant that they were heading somewhere that they were pretty sure that a bunch of women could reach on foot without fainting or collapsing. Somewhere close at hand, in other words. His horse would be fine where she was for a few hours so Archer set off after the raiders.

It wasn't a very long journey. The straggling group made their way along the road north, back in the direction that Archer and the nuns had been heading from yesterday. After no more than half an hour, they left the track and walked towards a rocky cliff which lay half a mile to the right of the road, running parallel to it for a space.

'Surely to God they ain't going to climb that cliff?' muttered Archer to himself, wondering what the hell was going on. He followed at a discreet distance. Without any warning, the troop of men and women seemed to vanish into thin air.

Archer speeded up a little and tried to see what had happened. To his amazement, he found a narrow gap in the cliffs, splitting them right down the middle. This formed a passage wide enough to take two men riding abreast. Very cautiously, he walked along this natural passage way. After a while, it opened out into what looked in the darkness to be a sort of natural amphitheatre, nestling in the hills. The rocky walls rose in gentle slopes around the whole place. Unless you knew where the entrance was, the chances of hitting upon this place by accident were more or less non-existent. Archer made his way very carefully up the slope to the right and when he had reached the top, settled down behind a boulder and waited for sun-up. We camped on their very doorstep, he thought. Fine scout I'm turning out to be for those poor women.

He drowsed fitfully in a sitting position, but was at once awake and alert as soon as first light came. The rising sun revealed an extraordinary scene. He was sitting on the upper slope of a circular depression in the hills. This saucer shaped valley measured perhaps a mile across and, as far as Archer could see, the only way in or out was from the narrow crevice through which he had entered a few hours earlier.

An encampment which was almost a

village lay on the floor of this curious geological feature. There were tents, wickiups and even one or two huts built from sun bleached wood. There was also a corral, holding twenty or thirty horses. Without doubt, this was the hideout or base of a gang of Comancheros. From his point of view, this was heartening, because he could work out what these fellows were about and what their plans were. These men earned their daily bread by trading with the Indians, preying on passing travellers and also by carrying out what was, to all intents and purposes, a slave trade. They kidnapped women and then sold them on to whoever would buy them. Presumably, this would be what they had in mind for Mother Veronica and her girls. Not, thought Archer grimly, while I've got breath in my body.

So great was his ability to sit perfectly still in one spot without moving in the slightest until the moment came to strike, that Lew Archer's old Army comrades used to josh him that he must have Indian blood running through his veins. He set himself up now, hunched behind the boulder with his rifle pointing down into the hidden valley. His breathing slowed right down and anybody watching him might have thought that he was on the verge of dozing off. It was nothing of the sort; he was merely conserving his energy, just setting quiet like a rattlesnake until it was the best time to strike.

It had been a good ten years since he had prayed, but Archer thought that no harm could come of giving it a shot now. He was by no means sure how the Lord might receive any petition of his, especially after such a long absence, but he didn't see that he had anything to lose by it. Besides, the Lord must surely be worried about the welfare of those four women, all of whom were devoted servants of his. So he composed his thoughts, took a deep breath and then uttered one of the strangest prayers which had ever been directed towards the Deity.

'Oh Lord, please set a watch upon those women down there and take care of them. I will do what I can to aid them, but I could surely do with some help from you. The odds are stacked against me and I hope that you can even them up in my favour a bit. I ask this in your son's name. Amen.' After having finished his own prayer, Archer thought that it would do no harm at all to follow up with one of the more conventional sort and so recited a Hail Mary.

A few slatternly looking women, half breeds by the look of them, were moving about the camp on various errands. Gradually, as he watched, the place came to life. There was no sign of the Sisters; Archer guessed that they were being held with other women in one of the larger wickiups. As he surveyed the little settlement, he tried to calculate how many men there were. His best estimate was between twenty and twenty-five. In addition to the men, were their amours or wives or servants, or whatever role was filled by the women who were doing all the domestic drudgery about the camp. Even if his lower estimate was correct, he was not going to be able to free those nuns after fighting single-handed against twenty men.

Archer ran through a few plans in his head in order to see which one was the best fit, given the circumstances. He was a crack shot with a rifle and his Springfield was an adaptation of the kind of musket he had carried in the war. It had just been converted into a breech loader; other than that, it was the self-same weapon. At a range of half a mile with this thing, he could shoot out the eye of a fly. But how many men could he kill in that way from up here, that was the question to be asking. He figured that he could probably fire ten rounds a minute with this rifle. That meant that if he opened fire now, without any warning, then he might kill half a dozen men before the others took cover and began firing back at him. That was no good, it would develop into a stand-off and he would still be outnumbered fifteen to one.

Another possibility would be waiting 'til dark and then sneaking down there and freeing the Sisters, hoping to smuggle them out of the village and back onto the road. But what then? Even if those oxen had not succumbed to thirst by then, they would still not be able to outrun the Comancheros on their fleet little ponies. That scheme wouldn't answer, either.

The sun was rising high in the sky and hot on the back of Archer's neck, when the nature of the problem changed and became enormously simplified. All the men seemed to be up and about by this time, talking and smoking. Nobody appeared to be in any kind of urgent hurry until a lone rider emerged from the entrance to their camp and galloped into the centre of the place. He spoke very excitedly, gesticulating and practically shouting at the men. Obviously, something was afoot. There was suddenly a lot of action with men running to and fro, fetching rifles and saddling up horses from the corral. Fifteen minutes after the rider had appeared, twenty of the men were mounted up and armed to the teeth. Then they trotted single file out of the valley.

Apart from the women moving about, Archer could now see that only three men had been left behind. One of these was little more than a boy, aged perhaps sixteen or seventeen at most. If he was going to act, then now was surely the perfect time. He would have to leave it long enough for the sound of his shooting not to carry on the wind to those who had left. Half an hour should do the trick. Archer took out six cartridges for the Springfield and lined them up ready on the rock in front of him. After he gauged that at least thirty minutes had passed, he took aim at one of the men below, who was fixing a tent. The other two were also in the open, which was important if he was going to be able to kill all of them in short order. Cocking the rifle, Archer squinted down the barrel and fired at the man by the tent. His bullet took the fellow right in the chest.

The instant he fired, Archer worked the breech to eject the old cartridge and then reloaded. The young boy was staring about him wildly, clearly not knowing where the shot had come from. Archer fired again, hitting the youngster clean through his head. Once more, he reloaded.

The third man was nowhere in sight and had obviously gone to ground. Archer scanned the area frantically, but there was no sign of the other man. The women were screaming and running around like headless chickens. There was no point waiting so Archer began running down the slope towards the wickiups and tents. He would just have to hope that none of the women were any great shakes with firearms.

As he skidded down the loose stones which covered the ground, Archer drew his pistol and cocked it. They really needed to move very quickly now if there was to be the least chance of pulling off their escape from here. He was hoping to get five horses tacked up, apart from anything else, and that was before he had even thought about how he would teach three or four complete novices to ride.

Archer reached the floor of the valley and looked about him cautiously. All the women had taken cover, either by throwing themselves to the ground or scuttling into the nearest wickiup or tent. He gazed around, desperately anxious to get moving and yet keenly aware that there was a man hidden down here who would be trying to put a bullet in him. He ran to the nearest tent and opened the flap with his rifle. Two dark skinned women, who looked like they might be either Indians or very sun-tanned Mexicans, regarded him fearfully.

'I ain't a going to hurt you,' he told them.

The next tent was empty. As he went

to look at a group of wickiups, there was a shot and the ball whistled so close to his head that he heard it buzz past his ear like an angry hornet. It was enough to give him a line on the whereabouts of the final man. Archer whirled around and fired four times with his revolver at the tent behind him from which he believed the shot to have come. There was no answering fire so he cocked the pistol again and ran over to see if he had killed his man. By some freak, two of his shots had been deadly; one passing right through the heart and the other smack bang between the eyes. It couldn't have been a neater job had the man been trussed up in front of him, ten feet away.

It was no time to stand around congratulating himself on his uncanny luck that day. He needed to track down the captive women and get them out of there. There was a whimpering, indicative of tremendous fear, from a nearby wickiup. Archer pushed the thing open and peered in, to find an Indian woman cowering in the corner and sobbing.

'Where are my friends?' he demanded. The woman tried to burrow into the earth, like a frightened jackrabbit. Archer bellowed at the top of his voice, 'Mother Veronica, where are you?'

From the other side of the encampment came a faint cry and he raced towards the source of the sound. There were other screams coming from the same direction. A large wickiup, the biggest in the place, seemed to be where the shouts were coming from and Archer ripped open the flap covering the entrance. The nuns were there and also two other white women. All had their wrists lashed together and a rope had been passed through those bonds and secured to a stout wooden post which was driven into the floor of the hut. Not for the first time in the last twenty-four hours, Archer felt himself being choked by a killing rage that any man could treat women so, stockading them as if they were cattle. He hoped that there would be a chance for reckoning with the beasts who had treated these women badly.

It did not take him long to draw his knife and slash the ropes binding the six women. As he was freeing them, he said to the Reverend Mother, 'Sister, we are going to have to leave right fast. Can you ride horse-back?'

'Yes, I have done when I was younger.'

One of the things that Archer had come to admire about Mother Veronica was that she never wasted words. Everything she said was to the purpose, with not a spare word used unnecessarily. This was rare enough in men and he had never yet encountered it in a woman. He said, 'I'm going to saddle up seven horses. You will all have to ride out of here. That means you and your girls riding astride, I'm afraid.'

Incredibly, even after all she and the others had been through, the Reverend Mother was still able to treat the matter lightly, saying, 'Yes, I doubt these chaps keep side saddles here.'

'Sister, will you get the ladies

organized, while I tack up some horses? I don't know how long we have. Not very long at all, I'll warrant.'

Without waiting for a reply, he stalked off and began ransacking the tents in search of saddles. He found seven and raced off to the corral to tack up some ponies. Although he chose the meekest looking of the dozen animals there, they still looked a lively enough crew. How the young nuns would manage them, he really had no idea.

Archer didn't want to waste more time putting on bridles and only fitted one on the horse that he himself intended to ride. He would be able to exchange this one for his own when they reached where they had camped the night before. Then at least one of the women would have reins to clutch at. He hollered over to the women and Mother Veronica shepherded them over to the corral. As soon as they were assembled, he said, 'All of you have to get up on these horses now. I don't care if you never sat on a horse before. I'll help you up and then you can just hold on by gripping the front of the saddle. It's the best I can do and we need to get out of here right this minute.'

Mother Veronica said to her girls, 'Come, Sisters, I will help you to mount.' The two other women looked to have some experience of horses and climbed up by themselves.

When the women were all on their horses, Archer said, 'We are going to proceed out of here at a walk. Just hang on to the saddle at the front and you will all be fine.'

He didn't want to give any of them the opportunity to object or claim that they didn't think that they would be able to do it, so he started off at once, leaving the Reverend Mother to get her charges organized. Then he led the way to the gap in the cliffs which gave access to the road beyond.

As the seven of them threaded their way between the narrow walls which enclosed the path to the valley, Archer began to ponder on the next step.

Anything other than a gentle walk was out of the question.

Glancing back, he could see at once that the young nuns were finding it enough of a challenge just to stay on their mounts at this pace. They surely wouldn't be able to venture a trot. Then there was the little matter of provisions. How far would his group be getting without food and water? If they managed until midday before the first of them fainted, he would be surprised.

Still and all, they were now free of the Comancheros' lair and that was something. With a little luck, those bastards might have left the water kegs untouched in the wagons and that at least meant that the women would be able to slake their thirst before they set off for the day. Archer scanned the horizon anxiously. He had not the faintest notion why all those men had left the valley, nor when they would return. More particularly, he could not adventure a guess as to the direction from which they would be coming home. For all he knew to the contrary, he and the women might be riding right towards them at this very moment. There was little enough that could be done about that, though.

Mother Veronica's thoughts had evidently been moving along the same line as his own, for she said at this point, 'Mr Archer, do you think those men left our water alone?'

'I hope so, ma'am, I'm sure,' he replied, 'else we are like to be in an even worse fix.'

'What do you hope for? That we can get to a town or something, before those bandits catch up with us?'

'I couldn't say. There's no sign of any town hereabouts and the road we've been travelling ain't exactly what you would call busy. If push comes to shove and those devils come upon us, then I guess I'll have to try and fight them off.'

'What was the shooting we heard? Did anybody die?'

'Well,' said Archer grimly, 'I didn't die, for which you may be thankful.'

When they reached the wagons, it was to find that the water kegs had been left alone and everybody drank as much as was wanted. Archer retrieved the palomino and let the youngest and most nervous of the nuns take the Comanchero pony with the bridle and reins. Before they set off again, he contrived to have a brief and private conference with the Reverend Mother.

'I will tell you straight, ma'am,' he said in a low voice, 'I don't fancy our chances here. We're going to be ambling along at a walk and those boys can gallop like the wind. They will be after us the second they get home and find what has happened. Apart from the death of their friends, you and your Sisters have a hard cash value to them.'

'Yes, I know all about that. Those two girls that were already in their camp have told me pretty much all that I need to know. One of them was the mother of that baby we saw. I had to break it to her that her child was dead, as well as her husband. She is almost out of her mind with grief.'

'What I wanted to say, Sister, was this. If there is sign of pursuit, then you and the others will ride on and I will engage to delay them as long as can be. That's all I can think of, unless you have any ideas of your own?'

'Nothing that comes readily to mind, Mr Archer.'

It was a warm morning and unless Archer was greatly mistaken, it would not take long before the lack of food and water began to affect one or other of the women. He had not the faintest idea what was to be done about this, but when he looked back to check how they were all managing, he saw something which drove all thoughts of refreshments clean out of his head.

On the horizon was a column of dust which told of a large group of riders heading towards them. He looked around the barren landscape, wondering if there was anywhere at all that they could hide. There was nowhere. He rode up to Mother Veronica and said, 'Here's where the knife meets the bone, ma'am. There's a bunch of riders coming up behind us. You take the others on and I will stay here and see what I might do.'

'No,' said the Reverend Mother decisively, 'I'll do nothing of the sort. It's madness.'

'It's the only plan on the table. 'Less you have a better one?'

'They'll just ride around you. You might get one or two, but that's all. And afterwards, we'll still be taken. We will stay together and hope for the best.'

It was quite clear that Mother Veronica was not going to follow his instructions and in a way, he felt glad. It would have been a lonely enough death, crouched behind a boulder here and being used for target practice by a bunch of bandits.

'Well then,' Archer said, 'since we can't outrun them, I suppose we might as well all dismount and see what chances next.'

As he peered hard into the distance, trying to work out if it was Indians or Comancheros riding down on them, Archer began to think his eyes were playing tricks upon him. For the harder he stared, the more it appeared to him that all the riders were somehow coloured blue. The explanation, when once it struck him, caused him to whoop with joy, to the great alarm of the young nuns. Even Mother Veronica looked a little taken aback and asked, 'Whatever is it, Mr Archer?'

'Why, ma'am, just you look at those boys coming up behind us. What do you see?'

The Reverend Mother shielded her eyes with her hand and watched closely. Then her own face creased in a smile. She did nothing as vulgar as whoop with joy, but she did call her nuns to her, saying, 'Girls, come here. The Lord has smiled upon us.'

By now, everybody could see plainly that a column of US cavalry was riding towards them. There looked to be more than enough of them, that even if the Comancheros did show up now, they were sure to be bested by the soldiers.

7

The look of amazement on the faces of the troopers was comical to behold. There was nothing for miles around and then suddenly they had stumbled across a group of nuns. Archer explained the case to the officer in charge who, like him, showed freely the disgust he felt for men who would traffic women in this way as if they were some sort of commodity.

There were sixty men in the column and, by great fortune, they were a mixture of regular troopers and men from the Commissary taking provisions to the troops stationed on the Rio Grande. This meant that in addition to the men on horseback, there were also twenty carts, carrying food, tents and all manner of supplies. The women were able to climb up onto these wagons and travel in ease. The cavalry were planning to stop over at a town just a day's ride away, called Sheldon. Major Fosdyke, who was in charge of the whole outfit, would not make any promises, but hinted that it might be possible to let Archer and his nuns travel south with them.

The turnaround in their fortunes was so marked, that Archer felt quite light-hearted as he rode alongside the wagon containing Mother Veronica. He said facetiously, 'Well, ma'am, the Lord certainly came up trumps that time. I was sure that we would either starve to death or be captured by those villains. Happen your prayers were answered.'

The nun was not in the least offended by his flippant manner, saying, 'That's how it is sometimes when you trust in God. Strange things do have a way of happening. By the by, I did not thank you properly for freeing us all from that camp.'

'Did you think I had cut and run?' asked Archer, half joking and half serious.

'Not a bit of it, Mr Archer. I don't see you as a man who would abandon his friends. No, I told my Sisters that you would be coming along directly and setting things straight for us. I said they could depend upon it.'

'Did you really?' he asked, a queer look on his face. 'Did you really tell them that you thought I would be coming for you all?'

'Of course I did. I never doubted it for a moment.'

It was a curious feeling to know that you were trusted so absolutely in that way. Curious, but exceedingly pleasant and warming to the heart. That such a person as the Reverend Mother should place implicit trust in a rogue like him made Archer determined to be a better person in the future, or at least to make some effort in that direction.

As far as he could make out, the Commissary people would be staying for two nights or more in Sheldon. This suited Archer well enough, because he felt that the nuns needed a bit of a rest after all their adventures. It would do them no harm at all, including Mother Veronica, to take things easy for a few days. For his own part, he had a deal of thinking to do about the future course of his life and he was looking forward to the chance to take breath a little and reason things through. Being called a thief had got under his skin and was worrying him like a cockleburr.

Sheldon, when it hove into view, seemed a nice, peaceful town. Some towns, as soon as you entered them, you could sense that you had to mind your Ps and Qs, unless you were actively seeking trouble. Others, like Sheldon, were as calm and relaxed as could be. It wasn't what one might term a large, bustling metropolis; there was only the one street, with houses and other buildings scattered on either side.

The cavalry proposed to camp near the town and offered the women a tent of their own, if they should want it. Archer hoped to find better diggings than that for the nuns and went straight into the town and hunted out the pastor of the local church. This worthy was not too keen on Catholics, judging from what he said. In fact, it sounded to Archer like he thought they were next door to being representatives of the Prince of Darkness himself.

'Catholic nuns, you say? Can't say there's like to be many wanting them here.'

'They're God-fearing women, on their way to start a school. They've had the devil of a time, taken prisoner by Comancheros and I don't know what all else. I'm asking you to find rooms for them for one night, two at the most. Ain't there Christians in this here town?'

The pastor did not take to being buffaloed like this. In the end, he told Archer to come back in an hour and he would see what might be done. In some of these little towns, as Lew Archer was well aware, the prevailing religious beliefs tended towards a fierce brand of

Protestantism, with the Pope in Rome being seen as more or less the Anti-Christ. It was enough that the pastor hadn't slung him out on his ear and had promised at least to see what he could do.

Back where the cavalry had halted, they were busily erecting their tents and setting up shop for the night. When Archer explained, with as much delicacy as he could, that there was a certain lack of enthusiasm for finding the four nuns rooms for the night, Mother Veronica caught his drift at once. The other two women he had rescued were happy to stay in a tent provided by the soldiers.

'With luck,' said Archer, 'you will be able to travel all the way down to the Rio Grande with the cavalry. I'm sure that they'll be able to take care of you a sight better than I've been able to do.'

'But you are still coming with us, are you not, Mr Archer?' asked the Reverend Mother, with what to Archer's ears sounded like a tinge of anxiety. 'I would not trust anybody but you to see us safely to our destination.'

'It's right nice of you to say so, ma'am — ' began Archer, before Mother Veronica cut in with asperity.

'It's not nice at all. I want to get to where we are going and you are the man to get us there. I don't altogether trust those soldiers, who have some game of their own going on. They are not devoted to our interests as you are, Mr Archer.'

'I guess our paths are still running alongside of each other for a while,' said Archer. 'Let's see what happens in a day or two.'

Since he had picked up with the nuns, Archer had found himself noticing things which he might not have done before. On his way back to see the pastor of the church, with a view to finding accommodation for the Sisters, he passed Sheldon's one and only saloon. A child was cleaning the floor and then sweeping the dust and forth out onto the road. This little fellow could not have been more than eleven or twelve, and from the look of him, was probably Mexican; maybe an orphan who was given a job like this in exchange for board and lodging. As the boy wielded the broom vigorously from the door of the saloon, he chanced to catch the shin of a man walking past. The child barely had time to stutter a few halting words, begging forgiveness for his clumsiness, before this man grabbed hold of his shoulder in annoyance and raised his hand in readiness to deliver a blow. He was mightily surprised to find his wrist gripped from behind and his arm twisted behind his back.

'You let that child alone, mister,' said Archer softly, 'he didn't bang your leg apurpose. You want to raise your hand to anybody, try me.'

The man turned angrily, ready for action, but something in Archer's eyes warned him that he was on the wrong road and he mumbled a hasty apology and hurried off. The funny thing was that Archer was not, as a rule, apt to involve himself in other folk's affairs like this and a month ago, he might not even have noticed such an incident; much less taken an active role in it himself.

The pastor grudgingly informed him that two of his flock could spare rooms for a couple of nights. It would mean the nuns doubling up, but there it was, there were two rooms if that was any help. Archer thanked the man profusely and hurried back to the army camp to pass on the glad tidings. As he neared the little group of tents, he passed four troopers who were standing around, idling and smoking. They were watching the youngest of the nuns, Sister Agatha, as she moved to and fro on some errand. One of the men made a coarse remark about the young girl, which prompted gales of laughter from his companions. Archer went up to the man at once and said, 'You want to watch that mouth of yours. It will trip you up one of these fine days.'

'What's it to you?' asked the man.

'It's this,' said Archer. 'I am looking after those ladies and anything touching upon them is my affair. Next time I hear anything filthy being spoken about them, I will not give warning, but settle the matter at once.'

The four soldiers looked at this scrawny young man and wondered what his connection with the nuns might be. They couldn't be brawling in camp or they would be in trouble so one of them ended the thing by saying to his mates, 'Ah, he's one of them holy types you hear tell of. Always praying and keeping himself pure. He's a regular missioner.' The others laughed and the tension broke. They walked off, ignoring Archer.

After they had gone, he thought to himself, is that how I seem to the world now? Like a man who's got religion? Lord, I hope not. That ain't me at all.

The Reverend Mother was pleased to hear about the rooms that would be available for her and her girls, and was not at all fussed that it would entail sharing.

'I dare say,' she said, 'that we will be obliged to endure a good deal more in the way of inconvenience when we get to the border than just not having a room each for ourselves. I am very grateful to you, Mr Archer. I truly do not know what we would have done without you.'

'It's nothing to speak of, ma'am. I'm only glad I could be of assistance.'

Archer didn't feel the need for either a tent or room that night and had a hankering to sleep out under the stars. After making provision for his horse, he took his saddle-bag and blanket out of the town and settled himself down where he had a little peace and quiet. The spot that he had chosen was a little to the north of Sheldon, only a stone's throw from the road along which they entered the town. It was only about eleven, but he felt pretty tired, having only dozed fitfully the previous night.

After he had wrapped himself up in the blanket and laid his head down on the saddle-bag, he became aware of the drumming of hoofs. It sounded to him like three or four horses heading towards him, presumably from the other direction to Sheldon. It was an odd time to be travelling a lonely road and he sat up to see if he could catch a glimpse of the riders.

The hoof-beats ceased and he heard the metallic jingling of bridles. As he read it, the men who had been riding into Sheldon in such haste had now stopped for some reason. Without making any sharp movement which might attract attention, Archer turned his head very slowly to see what he could, which in the pitch darkness was not much. He couldn't see much, but he could hear quiet conversation. Leastways, it started quiet and then rose in volume as the men began some species of disputation, which sounded like they were getting vexed with each other. Thing is, they weren't speaking English. They were using that same queer dialect of Spanish that he had heard twenty-four hours earlier, when the Comancheros had snatched the nuns from their wagons.

Archer rolled over and stealthily crawled forward. He was fifty yards or so from the men and although the figures were shadowy and indistinct, he counted five riders. Although he couldn't make any sense of what was being said, their manner and the tone of their voices was such as to convince him that here were men up to no good. He had heard enough men plotting mischief in the past to be sure that these chaps weren't discussing a picnic. They were angry and wanted to do something about it.

Reluctantly, Lew Archer rolled up his blanket and stashed it in his bag. Then he waited until the five horsemen had rode on into town and followed them at a brisk lope. It was a blasted nuisance, but he had a suspicion that this was apt to be another night when he didn't get much in the way of sleep.

8

It could not have been far short of midnight and most of Sheldon was tucked up quietly in bed. Only the saloon was still lit up and alive. Perhaps the fact that it was Saturday and many folk would be having a little lie in in the morning accounted for the saloon staying open later, but whatever the explanation, there was plenty of noise coming from the place; talking, shouting, laughter and even the discordant plinking of an old and poorly tuned piano. If the men who Archer had heard talking were strangers in these parts, then the saloon would probably be the first location for which they would be making a beeline.

He had his pistol ready and loaded and also the Springfield slung over his shoulder, but Archer was worried that all this weaponry might lend him a warlike and martial air and set off the very sort of trouble that he was trying to avoid. The Navy Colt flapping at his hip was one thing; many men hereabouts went heeled, even for an evening at the bar room. The rifle was something else again, though, and that really did give an aggressive impression, particularly at this time of night. He propped it up carefully in the darkened doorway of the general store, along with his saddle-bag. He would just have to trust to luck that nobody would meddle with it or make off with his other belongings. Hoping that he now looked like any other sodbuster, he approached the Silver Dollar saloon, pulled back the batwing doors and walked in.

There was a carefree and relaxed atmosphere in the saloon. There were only men in there, but everybody seemed amiable enough and just there for a sociable drink or two. As soon as he set foot in the place, Archer at once spotted the men who he had overheard talking on the road. At least, he could not actually recognize them; it had been too dark to get a good look, but there were five men standing at the bar and waiting to be served who stood out like the proverbial sore thumb. All the other men were wearing their good clothes and making a show of their good humour and general bonhomie. Not the group at the bar, though. They were a different breed entirely.

The five men were travel-stained and dusty, which in itself was somewhat of a breach of etiquette for a Saturday night in the saloon. Their rough clothes also marked them out. One could tell just from looking at these men that they had jumped on their horses and ridden hard for hours and come straight into the Silver Dollar after that ride, without so much as brushing their hair or washing their faces. Even without those clues, though, you could have seen that these men did not belong in this place and that they were perhaps unwelcome. Those standing near to them had moved a little away as they approached the bar, as though fearing contagion. Although the bar room was crowded, with men jostling and rubbing elbows amicably, a good three or feet separated this group of travellers from the rest of the drinkers present.

The barkeep did not seem in any great hurry to serve the newcomers, which provided Lew Archer with a few moments to weigh up the situation and figure how matters stood.

Without doubt, these must be some of the Comancheros whose camp he had raided that morning. It might be guessed that they had followed the track of their horses in this direction, although surely the column of cavalry would have obscured most such evidence? Maybe this was the nearest town so they assumed as a matter of course that any fugitives would be likely to fetch up here? That was more likely. Why had they come here? That was not a difficult question to answer. They could not be mad enough to think that they would be able simply to march into the town and snatch back the women he had freed. Gauged by the evil looks that they were receiving from the other patrons of the Silver Dollar, enough was known or suspected about these men to make them less than popular in the town. There were enough townsfolk carrying weapons as to make it a suicidal act for these five to try and make off with captives from Sheldon.

No, the explanation for their presence here this night was simplicity itself. They had been, as they saw it, cheated out of the profits to be made from the sale of six women and had also found three of their band killed dead. They were looking for revenge.

If these men had come looking for him three days earlier, then nothing would have induced Archer to fight them. He had a greater duty towards the nuns he was caring for. Now though, the case was altered. The nuns were safe here and the army would be letting them go along with them to the

Mexican border. You might say that Mother Veronica and her Sisters were provided for. Which meant that he, Lew Archer, pretty much had a free hand now. He had the opportunity to show these skunks just exactly what he thought about them and perhaps to teach them not to molest women another time. He walked towards the men still standing at the bar and waiting for the barkeep to take notice of them.

Archer had no intention of needlessly casting away his life and even as he approached the five desperadoes standing at the bar, his mind was racing furiously to work out the most effective way of accomplishing his end. As he neared the men, he veered slightly and slowed up a mite. The batwing doors of the saloon were now directly behind him at a distance of some twenty feet and he took his stand there, with the five Comancheros no more than twelve or fifteen feet in front of him. Then he just stood and waited.

The other drinkers had noticed the young man standing there, staring at the backs of the five men and gradually the chatter and noise died down as folk watched to see what his next move might be. Even the pianist sensed that something was afoot and stopped playing. The silence stretched out and one of the Comancheros glanced behind him uneasily. He saw Archer standing motionless behind him and then nudged his companions, who also turned around. The biggest and ugliest of the fellows, who Archer took to be their leader, said in a heavily accented voice, 'What you looking at? Are you looking for trouble?'

'Why,' said Archer mildly, 'isn't that the coincidence? I was just now on the point of asking you the self-same question.'

'We are looking for a man — ' began the leader of the Comancheros, before Archer cut in with a humorous twinkle in his eye.

'Hey, that is another big coincidence. They do say that the age of miracles has not ended. I'm looking for a man, too. I wonder if you are the one. Tell me now,' he continued in an affable and chatty way, 'who's this man you're looking for?'

The big man straightened up and took a few steps, which caused him to be standing facing Archer, so that they were barely six feet apart. 'I am looking for the bastard who killed my little brother. I have cause to think that the cowardly son of a whore and a black dog is hiding here in this town.'

'I don't reckon you need look a deal further. Would you be the low, creeping creature who has been selling women like they were cattle or something? I thought we'd been looking for each other.'

The Comanchero's face began twitching and he looked like he would go for his gun at once. This did not suit Archer at all. He said, 'It's plain murder and death to us both at this range. Why don't we both back off ten foot and then you get one of your boys to count to three?'

The other man gave an almost imperceptible nod of his head. The two of them began to back away from each other, both watching the other for signs of treachery; drawing and firing before the signal had been given. With a room full of witnesses, it would have been a foolhardy man who broke the rules of the duel. Archer had an idea that most of the men present would be happy enough to open fire on the bandits and those gentlemen probably knew it. A fair fight of this nature, though, was another thing and since it was just two men with a grievance against each other, settling the dispute in the time-honoured way, it was unlikely that anybody would intervene.

Both Archer and the leader of the bandits walked back until they could go no further, prevented by either the bar or, in Archer's case, the doors opening out onto the sidewalk. Then the two men stopped and waited, each eyeing the other with looks of loathing and detestation. One of the other men at the bar said loudly, 'One!'

Usually in such affairs, both participants are focusing all their mental energies on being ready to send their hand snaking down to the holster and snatch up the pistol nestling there. Lew Archer, though, was thinking of something else entirely. He was flexing his knees slightly and making sure that the muscles in his legs were supple and relaxed.

'Two!' cried the man who had taken upon himself the role of timekeeper.

Now Archer and his opponent were just watching each other's eyes, hoping to detect the least inclination to move before the final count of three. Archer's legs were now distinctly sagging at the knees and anybody examining him closely might almost think that he was on the verge of fainting.

'Three!' As the word was called, Archer allowed his knees to give way altogether. As he dropped to the ground, he kicked forward, sending his body sprawling at full length on the sawdust strewn floor of the saloon. As he went forward, he reached down and brought up the pistol, cocking it with his thumb as he did so. He had known very well that the bandit was apt to be faster on the draw than he was. All he could hope was to give himself an edge by this unorthodox move. Only thing was, would this be sufficient to throw the other man off kilter?

The Comanchero leader had fired instantly at the count of three, his bullet smashing through one wing of the saloon doors, just exactly at the level that Lew Archer's heart had been a fraction of a second earlier. The sudden crouching spring of the other man had taken him aback and he was fumbling to cock his piece again, when Archer's bullet struck him between the eyes.

He did not stop to see whether he had hit his target; Archer rolled swiftly to one side and then leapt to his feet and ran through the door. He did not stop to open the twin doors and as soon as he was outside, he jumped instantly to the left. It was just as well that he had done so, because a bullet came whistling past his head as he moved from the doorway.

From back in the saloon, Archer heard a low boom that he took to be a scattergun. Then he was sprinting along the street to the darkened porch of the general store, where he had left his rifle. It was not in general the sort of thing he did, but on this occasion he had left a cartridge in the breech of the weapon and it was the work of an instant to cock the thing and bring it up to bear on the brightly lit oblong which was the door of the Silver Dollar.

There was the sound of more shooting from inside the saloon and then two men came running out, guns in their hands. Both were members of that same group that lately Archer had crossed swords with and since he had a crow to pluck with all those fellows for the way that they had snatched the Sisters, he opened fire at once, dropping one of the men right in the middle of the street. The second man ran off, away from where Archer was crouched in the darkness.

There was no more shooting from the Silver Dollar so he took it that it was safe enough to pass the doorway. At a guess, the men in there had settled with the other bandits in one way or another. Archer set off in pursuit of the last man. Now what he could never have guessed was that Mother Veronica had been up and praying in the yard of the nearby house where she was staying. When she heard the shooting, she must have come running straight towards it, either because she thought she might be able to help the wounded or perhaps pray for the dying. They would never know what had motivated that good woman, but she stepped around the corner of the blacksmith's forge, right into the path of the fleeing Comanchero. Dressed as she was all in black, he could not have seen her until he nearly ran right into the shadowy figure which was apparently seeking to block his path. He acted instinctively and fired twice.

Coming up from behind the man, Archer could not at first see what had happened. He heard the shots, though, and very nearly tripped over the Reverend Mother's lifeless body, where it lay on its back in the roadway. He saw the robes and knew at once that this was one of the nuns, but the light was not good enough for him to tell which. Archer bent closer and in the gloom, discerned the still calm face of Mother Veronica, her eyes open and gazing up to heaven as though she were still at her devotions. He felt frantically for a pulse, but knew deep within that it was hopeless and that the brave and dedicated woman had left this worthless shell and was now seated at the Lord's table. Even though this was a cause for celebration and not grieving, Archer could not prevent himself from sobbing in dismay at the sight of the dead woman.

In the short time that he had known her, Mother Veronica had impressed him more than any person he had met in his life. He had met plenty of villains and rogues; she was the first genuine saint ever to cross his path. There was little to be done for her, other than to lift up her corpse and carry it over to the wooden boardwalk and lay it reverently down, closing the eyes and crossing the hands upon the breast. Not for all the money in the world would he have left the nun lying sprawled haphazardly in the road like that. Then he set off to hunt down her killer.

The man he was after had a good start on him now, but it was fairly clear that he would be trying to work his way around the outskirts of the town so that he could retrieve his horse and ride hard for that hiddle valley. Not while Lew Archer had breath in his body, he wouldn't. Archer ran as fast as he was able along a little lane which ran along the backs of the buildings which lined the main street. If he was right, then the man would be heading the same way, running parallel to Archer. As he reached the end of main street, he caught a glimpse of a shadow to his left, running fast and trying to keep low and out of sight. That was his man, for a bet.

Mind, Archer thought, I can't shoot down a running man, just on the off chance that he is a killer that I am chasing. I will at least have to challenge him and see what he does. His pistol was in his hand and he cocked it. How many shots had he already fired? Three or four? At best, he only had two left. He would have to make sure that he did not make any errors. Not only did he have it in mind to prevent this man from fleeing the town, he wanted to be sure that it was he himself who killed him. The death of the Reverend Mother was to him an intensely personal grief, which would in no way be assuaged by any courtroom trial or even lynching by the men of the town. This man was his alone.

It was a fair bet that the Comancheros would have left their horses a little way from the saloon and then walked in there. They probably wouldn't have wanted to ride, all five of them, up to the place, looking like a party of armed men bent on bloodshed. So Archer reasoned and so it proved, because he came upon five horses tethered to a post rail at the back of the livery stable. All that was needed now was to wait for the man to come and claim his mount.

The survivor of the little expedition had taken the long way around and as a result, Archer could hear his breathless panting before the man himself came into sight. He drew down on the sound and then called into the darkness, 'I'm waiting for you, you son of a bitch. Did you think you were going to get away?' This was a fair challenge and if this was an innocent person, he would give him a chance to explain himself. As it was, the only reply to his words were two shots, both of which went wild. Archer kept quiet, with his pistol aimed where the flash of the shots had flared in the night. He wasn't about to shoot blind, though, not knowing that he might have only one charge left. He stood there and carried on waiting. After a minute, he heard a furtive creeping near the horses. A figure was fiddling around by the fence, probably untying one of the creatures. Then the man mounted his horse, throwing him into silhouette against the sky.

'Hidy!' said Archer and fired at once. The frightened horse went galloping off into the darkness, carrying the rider with it. Archer was quite sure that he had hit the man in the chest and thought that this probably closed the business for good. He holstered his weapon, walked back into the main street and went back to see what had been happening at the saloon since he had left.

There was quite a crowd outside the Silver Dollar. Most of them looked to be those who had lately been drinking there, but there were also men who had, by the look of them, thrown on clothes in a hurry when they heard the shooting and rushed from their homes to see what was to do. Most of them were clustered around the body of the man Archer had shot when he ran from the saloon, but down the street a way, he could see another crowd developing at the spot where he had laid out the body of the Reverend Mother. Some of the onlookers outside the saloon recognized him and urged him to go into the Silver Dollar for a drink, saying that he had earned it. This was heartening. Often under circumstances of this kind, you didn't know if the locals were going to congratulate you or string you up from the nearest tree. At least nobody here seemed to be ill disposed towards him for the shooting he had begun in their saloon.

Inside the Silver Dollar, three bodies had been laid on tables, one of which was the man he had himself killed. Of the other two, one was in a terrible state, with the head a bloody and formless mass. Archer learned later the reason for this. After he had dived out of the door of the saloon, the four remaining living Comancheros had drawn their guns and the barkeep, seeing that a shootout was well nigh inevitable, had taken the sawn-off shotgun which he kept beneath the bar and blown off the back of the head of the man standing nearest to him. Two of the other men had made it through the door, but the other of the party had drawn and turned to the barkeep, whereupon he had promptly been shot by one of the townsfolk drinking there that night.

All in all, what with nobody from the town being killed or even wounded during the brief gun battle, people were regarding the episode as an entertaining spectacle. Nobody had any love for men like that who would grab women and sell them into slavery, and Archer found himself applauded as something of a hero. This was even more the case, when it was discovered that he had accounted for the rest of the gang as well.

There was naturally a good deal of shock and dismay expressed about the death of a woman and a nun at that. Still, she too was an outsider and although her death was much to be regretted, things could have turned out a lot worse. Soldiers from the camp on the fringes of Sheldon arrived while Archer was listening to the explanations of what had been going on after he left the saloon. The cavalry too appeared not to be too distressed to hear of the death of some of those responsible for running women across the border. It was a filthy trade and there was not one person there that night who expressed a word of sympathy for the dead men.

After a while, Archer had had enough of it. He was not sorry to have killed the three men, but he did not glory or exult in their deaths. They had been like wild beasts and if you live that sort of life, then it is a fair bet that you will not die quietly in bed of old age. But even so, they had been men and it was a fearful thing to take lives in this way. Archer had killed enough people in the war that he was not squeamish about it, but he half wished that it had fallen to someone else to shoot those dogs down. He bade goodnight to various men and declined an offer of a free room at the saloon. He wanted to be by his self that night.

After fetching his pack from where he had left it by the store, Archer went out into the fields again and this time walked far enough that he could neither see nor hear any sign of the town. Then, before he huddled up in his blanket, he prayed for the second time since meeting the nuns. He knelt on the stony ground and said, 'Lord, we have not spoke properly for a good long while and maybe you are a mite vexed with me for steering clear of you for so long. I want to thank you for the help that I have received from you these last few days. I don't reckon I could have got by without but that you was looking down and aiding me at odd times.

'Please be sure to take up Mother

Veronica and not bother with purgatory or any such foolishness. She deserves to go straight to heaven. I guess you are wanting me to take those other three nuns in my care and see them safe to the border. I will do my best and then I hope you will show me what steps you would be wanting me to take next. Being a thief is no living for a man as he grows older. Amen.'

Then he wrapped the blanket around himself warmly and fell asleep almost immediately.

9

When he woke the next day, Archer had a good feeling about things. True, he had started the fight which had resulted in six deaths, but then those men had been set on mischief anyway; there would have been fighting regardless of what he did. At least as things had turned out, he was alive and they were dead. He felt great sadness at the death of Mother Veronica, but she was perhaps in a better place now. He rolled up his blanket, stuffed it into the top of his bag, picked up his rifle and walked back to Sheldon.

Archer found that he had achieved fame of a kind. Although it was a Sunday, Main Street was bustling and a few people nodded to him or wished him, 'Good morning'. The centre of attention that day was the Silver Dollar and he soon saw why. The bodies of the five Comancheros had been collected together and laid out on the boardwalk outside the saloon. Everybody in town looked to Archer to be keen on examining the corpses and discussing everything about them, from the expressions on the faces of the dead men, to the style of their clothes. There was, it seemed to him, something more than a little ghoulish about such goings on.

He was more concerned to find out what had become of the Reverend Mother and hoped that nobody had been crass enough to leave her body on public display. Archer needn't have worried. Making a show of a posse of bandits was one thing; a dead woman, something else again. Mother Veronica had been gently laid in a nearby shed and the door locked. He supposed that it would be up to him to make the necessary arrangements for her burial, although how that would work, he had no idea at all.

While he was wrestling with this difficulty, which had only just now occurred to him, he met the three younger nuns walking along the street. They looked, unsurprisingly, very melancholy. Archer, already having conceived it as his duty to take care of them until they reached their eventual destination, hailed them soberly and said, 'I know that this is the deuce of a thing to have happened, but we need to talk on the next step.'

The three girls looked at him apprehensively, without uttering a word. He saw that this wouldn't do at all so he set out what was on his mind. They could hardly be travelling together and making any sort of plans if these young women wouldn't even speak to him.

'Listen up now,' he told them, 'I can see that all three of you are broken up and bowed down by grief and suchlike. Very right and proper, too. I am also sorrowed by the death of the Reverend Mother. Mind, that's nothing to the purpose now. We need to make plans and I can't do that if none of you ladies will even speak to me.'

The three girls stood staring at him

mutely and Archer felt that he would need to take a more robust approach to this question.

'You there,' he said, pointing at the girl in the middle, 'You're Sister Agatha, is that right?' She nodded in a scared way, putting Archer in mind of a little fawn about to be seized by a mountain lion. 'Listen, I don't bite. I'm just a little rough and ready, is all. Your Mother Veronica wasn't affeared to talk to me and there's no earthly reason why you all should be, either.'

Still, the three frightened girls eyed him nervously. He said, 'Right now, tell me your names. Start with you on the right, there.'

'Sister Theresa,' said the nun, almost in a whisper. The other two vouchsafed their names to Archer and he felt like he was making progress.

'Well now, why don't the three of you come over with me to that log and you can all set there while I unburden myself to you and let you know where I stand.'

When the women were sitting side by side and gazing up at him fearfully, Archer said, 'You might know that I did not see eye to eye with the late Reverend Mother about the wisdom of this whole enterprise. Meaning which, I think it was a mad scheme for you all to be coming down here like this. Now I have the money that Father Joseph collected to pay for this school. I think that the best to be done is to get the three of you back to your convent and scrap the whole thing. Use the money for the poor or something similar.'

When he had finished giving his views and opinions to the nuns, Archer looked at them as though expecting nods of agreement at the wisdom of his advice. Instead, to his consternation, he met looks of the same mulish obstinacy as he had already seen several times on the face of their superior. Sister Theresa, who was apparently the next best thing that they had to a leader, said quietly, 'If you don't wish to come with us, Mr Archer, that's fine. Let me have the money that you are holding for us and we will continue by ourselves.'

'What do you other two have to say about it?' asked Archer, a little irritably. 'You both dead set on going south still?'

Both girls nodded and mumbled assent.

'Well, all I can say is that it's a blasted nuisance,' exclaimed Archer, 'a blasted nuisance. Nothing I can say to change your minds, I reckon?'

The three of them shook their heads apologetically, but he could see that they were as set on their course as Mother Veronica had been. 'Well, in that case, I guess that we are stuck with each other for a bit longer. The army are going to move tomorrow, from all that I'm able to collect. I think the Major will let us go with him. I shouldn't think that any of you girls want to ride, not if you can go in wagons?'

They shook their heads and two of the nuns had the beginnings of smiles flickering around the corners of their mouths. Well, thought Archer, that's a beginning at any rate.

'I'm going over to see the pastor,' he said. 'We must see about having Mother Veronica buried. I don't look to find a Catholic priest in this here town. Truth to tell, they don't seem to go a whole lot on Catholics in this neck of the woods. If I get the pastor to help out, do you suppose you girls will be able to make do by adding your own prayers and so on?'

The proposal was such an unusual one, that none of them looked as if they knew what to say. Archer didn't blame them one little bit; it's not every day that you are asked about the possibility of taking an active role in an impromptu funeral.

The pastor of the little church was more agreeable than Archer had expected. He was a decent man and looked to be truly shocked at the death of the nun.

'I think we can arrange a coffin at short notice,' said the pastor. 'It's a long story, but it so happened that we have one in the church. I hear where you and your charges are heading south tomorrow morning.'

It sounded right strange to Archer to hear the man describe the three nuns as his 'charges'. Lord knew what he made of the whole thing.

'That being so,' continued the pastor, 'I can get a grave dug in our burying ground this afternoon and we can have the funeral in the evening. Would that suit?'

'It surely would and I am grateful to you, sir.'

'There's no need. It's a terrible thing that has taken place. I understand that you played a part in the gun battle yesterday?'

'That's right,' said Archer, 'But I'd sooner not talk of it, if you don't mind.'

'Of course, of course. Shall we say that the funeral will be at five?'

'I'm sure that will be fine. Thank you again. Do we owe . . . ?'

'No, no, of course not. I'm glad to be able to help in such a sad case.'

As he left the church, Archer reflected that you never knew about folk and that was a fact. Yesterday, he had been sure that this man was a regular one for hating Catholics and now here he was, offering to provide a free funeral. It only goes to show, he said to himself, that you should not be hasty in judging others.

Major Fosdyke had the air about him of a man who had been expecting Archer. 'Oh, it's you, hey?'

'It looks that way,' replied Archer, nonchalantly. 'Are you still all right with me and my nuns travelling along of you when you head south tomorrow?'

'As far as it goes, yes.'

'What d'you mean, as far as it goes?'

'There's a whole heap of fighting going on twenty miles east of here. At least, that's what we've been told.'

'Who's fighting who?' asked Archer.

'Kiowa and Comanche fighting us, which is to say another cavalry unit. Our troopers are needed there, more than they are down on the border.'

'How does that leave things?'

'Forty men are riding east later today to provide reinforcement. My Commissary wagons are going south with twenty men. If your nuns want to ride the wagons, I have no objection.'

'I'm sure that they would be pleased to hear that, sir. I can ride alongside on my own mount.'

Having settled this to his satisfaction, Archer was about to leave, when the Major asked, 'What's all this I hear about you shooting some of those bandits last night?'

Archer gave a brief account of the battle, ending it by saying, 'I didn't go for to kill them, but by God, if any men deserved to die, I should just about say it was them fellows.'

'I'm of the same opinion,' said the Major warmly. 'Well done. They were engaged in a vile trade and they've only themselves to blame if decent folks show their dislike in so practical a form. I wish I could have shot one myself.'

Archer had been the cause of more

than one or two deaths by shooting since he had left the Army, but these were the first where everybody concerned was happy about the business. As he walked back to town, every man he saw touched his hat or said some cheery words such as, 'Smart work!' or 'Well done for ridding the town of those rats.'

Now what with all the excitement of the shooting at night and having to arrange for funerals and travelling plans and all the rest of it, Archer suddenly realized that he had not eaten a bite for close on twenty-four hours. He was used to skipping meals in this way, although not often for as long as a whole day. The only location in Sheldon which looked to be providing cooked meals for the general public was the Silver Dollar and so he made his way there.

The dead bandits were still lying in front of the saloon and although they had in life been the lowest form of crawling reptiles, Archer couldn't help thinking that they deserved some respect in death. So when he went into the saloon and up to the bar, he said to the man who served him, 'How much longer you going to leave those bodies outside like that? Kind of morbid, don't you think?'

'Well, sir,' said the barkeep, 'it's bringing in the trade.'

He gestured around the saloon. Although it was a Sunday and they were not serving liquor, the bar room was packed with customers. Some were eating, while others were sipping soda. All were discussing the exciting events of the previous night. When Archer had collected and paid for a plate of pork and beans, he was invited to several tables, where men were eagerly making room for him. They wanted to hear first-hand what had taken place here.

There was, at least to Archer's way of thinking, something rather disgusting about this avid curiosity for details of bloodshed and death. He had killed his share of men, but never felt like talking about the deaths later and had not the slightest interest in hearing about other men's killings. There it was, though. Strange as it might be, the folk in Sheldon regarded him as some species of hero for what he had done.

'Tell me, sir,' asked an elderly man with a white moustache, 'weren't you afraid of being killed yourself? They say you were as cool as a cucumber.'

'Any man says he's not afraid at such a time, he's either a liar or a mad fool. Sure I was afraid.'

'Yet you didn't show it, from all that I have heard,' pressed the man. 'They say you shot dead three of these scoundrels all by your own self.'

'That's true enough, I reckon,' said Archer. 'Mind, if they had killed me, I dare say you'd all be telling each other what a damned fool I'd been for taking on five at once.'

'Not a bit of it, my boy. If nothing else, we would have said that you were a brave fool.' Which caused Archer to laugh out loud and cheered him up somewhat.

After a time, the men around him fell to talking between themselves and left him to his own thoughts. Chief among these was how he, Lew Archer, was to help those shy young women set up their school. Without even thinking overmuch about it, he had come to the conclusion that he could not just deliver them to the Mexican border and then head back again. That Mother Veronica now, she was the one who could have sorted everything out without his help. If she had been spared, then he could have cut sticks as soon as they arrived near to the Rio Grande. But those three? He just knew that they would be like lost lambs without somebody to set things up for them and tell them what was what.

After considering this for a while, he felt that he really ought to check on the nuns and see that they didn't need anything. Not to mention where, Archer recalled suddenly, he had not told the girls about the arrangements for the Reverend Mother's funeral. He excused himself to those sitting around him and stood up to leave. One of the men said, 'Hey, what is it with you and those nuns? You're not a priest or some such, are you?'

'Not hardly,' said Archer, flashing a grin at the man. 'Nothing at all in that line.'

He didn't know where the young women were lodging and went to the church to enquire of the pastor. Archer found that gentleman engaged in digging the grave.

'I shoulda thought that you had somebody could do hard work like this for you,' he said. 'If you've another spade, I'll dig along with you.'

The pastor went off and returned with a second spade and the two of them set to work. After they had been digging for ten minutes, the pastor said, 'I don't recollect that you said how come you're escorting those nuns. You're not a churchman or anything, are you?'

'You're the second man to ask me

that in the space of an hour,' said Archer. 'I'll allow that it must look odd, a single young man like me in the company of three nuns. Still, there's nothing to the case really.'

He gave a brief outline of the events which had led to him teaming up with the Sisters. The two of them paused for a rest and the pastor said, 'That is a most remarkable tale. I don't know that I ever heard of such a stranger. What do you do when you're not undertaking this type of game? Meaning that is, what is your trade or profession?'

'Can't rightly say as I have one,' replied Archer, 'other than playing cards. But lately I've been thinking that is no way for a man to earn his living. I will have to take up something else.'

The two men took just over an hour to dig Mother Veronica's grave, making it a good, deep one. By the end of the job, they were both winded.

'I almost forgot,' Archer said, 'can you tell me where those girls are staying? I need to tell them what we have planned, as touching upon the funeral of their Mother.'

The pastor gave him directions to the two houses and Archer, after having thanked him warmly for his kindness in the matter of the Reverend Mother's funeral, took his leave.

Sister Agatha and her fellows were at home, being given a meal by the old woman with whom they were lodging. According to the old couple where Sister Theresa had been staying with the Reverend Mother, the Sister had taken a walk out into the fields. They opined that the older woman's death had hit the girl badly, which Archer had already suspected.

Sister Theresa was visible as a black dot in the distance and Archer set off after her. When he caught up with her, she did not appear to be all that pleased to have her solitude disturbed. Also, thought Archer shrewdly, she was perhaps not best pleased to find herself alone with a man. He tried to reassure her.

'Sister, now that the Reverend Mother has gone, I guess that you are kind of in charge of the other two. Is that how it is?'

'In a way,' she said quietly, 'although we are equals really.'

'Whether or no, I need to be able to talk over plans with somebody, the way I did with Mother Veronica. Should it be you or one of the others?'

'I will do.'

'Well then, here's the play. The funeral is to be held at five this very evening. Tomorrow, we are going to join up with those boys from the Commissary Department and they will take us south, carrying you and the others in their wagons. I have thought it over and can't decide if that will be safer or more dangerous for us.'

The girl looked at him as though he was mad. 'How could it be more dangerous?' she asked in a stronger voice than Archer had yet heard her use.

'Because of the fighting with the

Indians. They hate the bluecoats and will kill them wherever they can find them just now.'

'We didn't seem so safe when those men took us. I would rather be with the Army.'

'Well, Sister, so you do have opinions of your own, after all. I am glad to know it. And I agree with you. I think we are better being in the company of soldiers. I was just ravelling a thread and weighing up both sides.'

Sister Theresa said nothing more and Archer felt that she wanted to be alone. He reminded her that the funeral would take place at the little burying ground behind the Presbyterian church at five. Then he went back to town.

All the cards were falling just right; at least as far as Lew Archer could tell. They were guaranteed an escort of soldiers to their destination, he had the $3,000 safe and sound and, with a little good fortune, they would reach the border in less than a week. He wondered whether or not he should be buying provisions for the journey or if the Major would allow them to share the army's food and drink. He remembered the burning of the books out of the nuns' wagons as well and was possessed again of that impotent fury at the sheer stupidity of those bandits. He wasn't really at all sorry that he had shot those men; they surely did deserve it.

The funeral was, to Archer's enormous surprise, very well attended. Since the only church in town was Presbyterian and the dead woman had been a Catholic and quite unknown to anybody in Sheldon, he could not have imagined that any of the folk from town would be wanting to come to the ceremony. He had not counted on the morbid curiosity of those living thereabouts. The shootout had been a tremendously exciting and wholly unexpected event for Sheldon and a woman dying violently was in any case a great novelty and quite unheard of.

Whatever the reason, the burying

ground was crowded with both men, women and even a number of children. Many of the people had already been dressed up for church, it being a Sunday, and those same clothes were suitable for a funeral.

The pastor had spoken to the Sisters before the service. He might not have been too fond of Romish ways, but he recognized devout and God-fearing women when he met them. The consequence was that he left out of the standard burial service any parts calculated to offend a Papist and included one or two passages and prayers that the nuns had suggested.

After the pastor had said his piece, the nuns each led the crowd in a few prayers on their own account. This made a pleasant change for most of those present, it was like getting two services for the price of one. Then everybody filed past the open grave, each person casting a stone or clod of earth onto the coffin which lay at the bottom of the grave.

After everybody else had left, Archer made a point of speaking to the pastor and thanking him again for being so good about this. His thanks were brushed aside. As he was leaving, the man asked him, 'Tell me, what are you really about with those nuns? You told me the story, but there's something missing. Are you planning to stick with them once you are all down by the Rio Grande?'

'I can see where it looks kinda odd,' said Archer, 'And I won't pretend otherwise. Truth is, I don't know myself what I purpose. You could say my life has taken an unlooked for turn.'

After a discussion with the Sisters, Archer thought it best to buy some food for the journey. It was good of the Major to offer them hospitality on the way south and he didn't want to take too much for granted.

10

The Army wagons were not setting off too early and there was time enough the following morning for Archer to round up the Sisters, buy food and ensure that the four of them arrived at the encampment well before the men there were ready to strike camp.

Despite the idea being that they would be safer travelling in a column of cavalry, Archer couldn't help thinking that the line of supply wagons looked awfully vulnerable. Now that the fighting men had left, those remaining looked to his practiced eye to be either civilian cooks or clerks. This was, of course, not to be wondered at; after all, they were all members of the Commissary department, but Archer could not help wondering uneasily what sort of resistance these men would be able to put up if they were ambushed. Apart from the Major, there were only six men in uniform. His fears were allayed to some extent when Major Fosdyke confided in him.

'There should be another troop of our boys coming up to meet us. Like as not, we should not be long on the road before they join us.'

'Tell me, what sort of supplies are you carrying to the border?' asked Archer. 'I see a lot of crates and suchlike. Is it food, cooking utensils or what?'

'I'm afraid I can't discuss that,' said the Major, a little stiffly. 'Now if you'll excuse me, I have a lot to do today.'

If that wasn't an evasive answer, then Archer didn't know what was. It was no affair of his, but now that he knew that there was some mystery about the contents of the wagons and carts, he knew that he would not rest until he had solved it. There was no hurry, though. The journey would take about five days and he would have ample opportunity during the course of that time to poke about and find out what the Major was being so evasive about.

The nuns were in a good mood today and in as far as such modest, grave and reserved young women could be thought of as such, they seemed a little gay and light-hearted. At any rate, they smiled shyly at Archer, wished him a good morning and chatted among themselves almost like any other girls of that age. The train of carts left Sheldon just before midday and began wending its way south across the plain.

The next four days passed pleasantly enough. The men who he had in his mind dismissed as being like a bunch of cooks and clerks, proved to be anything but. The more he got to know them, the more Archer had the feeling that these men were specialists of some sort. They did not look like ordinary fighting soldiers, but that wasn't to say that they were soft or like civilians. They drove the wagons, cooked the food and took their turn at sentry-go each night, but these were men who played their cards close to the chest. He gained the impression that they were on some kind of mission, about which nobody was supposed to know. Whatever it was must be tied up with whatever it was being transported to the Mexican border and as the days passed, Archer became more and more determined to find out what was the case with all those heavy crates.

There was no sign of the column that was supposed to be meeting them from the south, but that did not look as though it signified. Everything was quiet enough in this part of the country and if there really was fighting going on with the Comanches, then it was not in this vicinity.

On the fourth evening since they had left Sheldon, Archer's curiosity finally got the better of him. He waited until everybody was sitting around, eating the evening meal and then crept off quietly in the evening gloom to sneak a closer look at one of the wagons. This one was loaded with pinewood boxes of varying sizes, with no markings or other distinguishing features. This in itself was an odd thing. The Army had an absolute mania for stamping their mark upon everything from horses and tents to the very pants worn by private soldiers. In all his years in the army, Archer did not ever recollect seeing crates like this without numbers or symbols stamped or burned onto them.

He drew the heavy Bowie knife that hung from his belt and used it to prise open the lid of the nearest box. The nails holding it down screeched in protest and he stopped at once, fearful that the noise would draw attention. Nobody came running, though, and he very carefully worked the lid loose and peeped beneath it. It was full of machine parts, each wrapped neatly in greaseproof paper. He pulled one out and examined it carefully. It was part of a Gatling gun. He gently pressed down the lid of that crate and tried another, which contained wooden kegs of powder.

Having ascertained the contents of two of the boxes, it was a fair guess that the others also contained ordinance of various types; powder and shot, Gatlings and who knew what else. Archer walked back and joined the others. His mind was working furiously.

He knew enough about the workings of the Army to know that there was something highly irregular about this consignment of arms. For one thing, this wagon train was posing as a transport of the Commissary, but that was a heap of nonsense if ever he had heard it. The commissary did not handle weapons or anything of that nature. Their role was limited to chuck wagons, paymaster's details, saddles, horseshoes and practically anything else that was not directly related to ordinance. Whoever these people were that he and the Sisters were travelling with, they were definitely not a routine Commissary detachment.

That night, as he lay awake, staring into the diamond-dust scattering of stars which crossed the vault of the sky, Archer worked out the whole thing. These weapons and whatever else they were carrying down to the border were nothing to do with the regular Army at all. They were probably going to ship them across the Rio Grande and hand them over to rebel groups in Mexico. Archer wasn't the most political of men, but he had heard about the Army 'losing' a lot of weapons to Juarez's forces, allowing him to overthrow the French soldiers occupying the country. There was plainly another such game being played now. He had thought it strange that the Army should be stationed down there, just so that they could, according to the story given out, stop all those refugees flooding across the border into the United States.

Having reasoned the matter out in this way, he wondered if there was anything that he ought to do about it. Did the presence of all those weapons, being carried secretly to the border, make the situation of the nuns any more hazardous? Might they be better off splitting away from the Army now and making their own way? How that might work, Archer had no idea at all. They didn't have any carts of their own now and he could hardly expect those women to walk the rest of the way; a distance of some thirty miles as far as he could calculate.

Waking early in the morning, Archer saw that only the Major and one or two other men were yet up and about. He pulled on his boots and approached Major Fosdyke. He said, 'I'm worried about those Sisters travelling like this with a lot of weaponry. Are you sure you're not like to be ambushed or attacked for those guns?'

'No,' said the officer, 'I'm not sure at all about that, Archer. This is an Army unit and we are fighting a war around here, in case you hadn't noticed. I said that you and those girls could join us when we headed south. I never said you had to do so.'

'Don't get all riled up,' said Archer soothingly, 'I am right grateful for your help. You can't blame me for worrying, though. It is up to me to look after those girls.'

'Anyhow, who said we're carrying ordinance? Has one of the men been talking out of turn?'

'Not a bit of it. I snuck a look in a few of your crates last night.'

'Oh you did, did you?' said the Major wrathfully. 'Well, sir, you have a damned nerve. That's all. What do you mean by it?'

Archer smiled disarmingly at the man. 'I was in the Army myself for better than four years. I could tell there was something not right about this.'

'I'll level with you, Archer, because I don't want to see ill befall those nuns of yours. Our General Sheridan was a damned fine officer in the late war, but he's dealing with the Indians now like he's still fighting a war against a regular Army. The Kiowa and Comanche are running rings round him. I don't look for you to repeat this to anybody, mind.'

'I think I know enough about useless Generals. I seed enough of my friends die because of the way that officers sat in comfortable quarters and gave bad orders.'

'Yes, well, you and me both. Anywise,

the General is setting up proper lines and I don't know what all else and the Indians are riding in from behind, right where they aren't expected. Between you and me, the whole campaign is a nightmare. Sheridan's supposed to be driving them around the state, but to many of us it looks like the boot's altogether on the other foot and they are driving us out.'

'I didn't know things were that bad.'

'They're bad enough. And now we are getting orders from Washington to arm rebels across the river in Mexico. Like we have not got enough to keep us busy already.'

'I appreciate you being so honest, Major. I reckon if it's all right by you, we'll stick with you for now.'

'Tell me, Archer, what is it between you and them nuns? You're not a priest or anything and yet you are taking as much care of them as if you were working for the Pope in Rome. How does that come to pass?'

'Tell you the truth, I ain't figured out

the finer points of that myself yet,' said Archer, with a rueful note in his voice. 'It is a mystery even to me!'

After breakfast, Archer led the Sisters aside and spoke earnestly to them. He said, 'I have been having some talk with the leader of the soldiers. Now I hope it comes to nothing, but I need to know that the three of you trust me.' He looked at each of the girls in the eyes. 'What I want is to be sure that all of you will follow my instructions if there is any emergency.'

The three of them looked at him without speaking. He said briskly, 'Come now, it's no difficult thing. I need only to have your word that if something happens, you will all of you do as I say at once, without any debate.'

Sister Theresa said, 'I can promise you that, Mr Archer. So will my Sisters here. Do you fear danger?'

'I don't rightly know what I fear, Sister. I found out one or two things last night and heard a thing or two this very morning. The consequence is that

I am uneasy in my mind and want to make sure that whatever befalls us, I can take care of you all.'

'Thank you,' said Sister Theresa, 'and thank you on behalf of us all.'

The road had led them so far across dry and dusty plains. The autumn rains had not yet come and the land looked parched. Now they were moving towards a line of hills which straddled the horizon. Unless he was very much mistaken, Archer thought that once they had passed through those hills, then they would be in sight of their destination. He was beginning to think that he had been worrying needlessly, turning into an old woman, fussing about things that would never come to pass.

The day wore on and by late afternoon, the line of wagons had reached the craggy cliffs which fronted the hills. The road meandered between a couple of the taller of the hills. They were not all that high, but rose almost vertically from the plain, giving them the appearance of miniature mountains; each about a hundred feet in height. It was at this point, just as they were on the point of passing into the rocky defile which led through this range of outcrops, that Archer turned back and saw what he at first took for rain clouds gathering behind them. Before he could remark upon this, the driver of one of the wagons muttered an oath and then shouted urgently to the Major. When the officer rode over, the man said to him, 'We got uninvited guests. Look over yonder.'

The two men looked at the cloud and then the Major called out for a halt. Everybody stared back across the wide plain. This was no storm cloud approaching, but was rather yellowish and billowed up from the ground. It was a mass of riders kicking up dust. The Major peered through his binoculars, before announcing, 'It's not the US cavalry, that's for sure.'

'How can you tell?' asked Archer. 'You surely can't pick out individual men at this range?'

'They aren't moving in line,' said

Major Fosdyke shortly. 'Whoever those riders are, they are coming on as a disorganized mass.'

One of the other wagon drivers said, 'Think we can outrun them?'

'Not a hope,' responded the Major, 'they are travelling fast and will be on us in an hour or two at the most.'

'You think they're following us?' asked Archer.

'I shouldn't wonder. This would not be the first consignment of weapons that was seized by the Kiowa.'

'How could they know what you're carrying?' said Archer. 'They don't have an intelligence service, do they?'

The Major laughed mirthlessly. 'They may as well do. We employ Indians as scouts. I don't doubt that they pass on information to their friends and relatives. Be that as it may, we must prepare.' He signalled for the wagon train to continue forward, up into the hills.

Archer rode after the Major and said, 'I thought we couldn't outrun them. What are you about?'

'I'm going to establish a defensible position up in those hills. It will be sheer murder if we're caught out on level country like this. Now if you'll excuse me, there is much to be done.'

The officer's face had a sheen of sweat and he was paler than usual. If Archer knew anything about fear, then this was a man in terror of his life, but trying valiantly to conceal the fact.

There was still at least an hour for him to plan what was best for his charges and Archer simply rode alongside the wagons, wondering what would be for the best. If he had only his own life to consider, he would certainly have thrown in his lot with the soldiers; nothing would have induced him to cut and run like a coward. But this was a different griddle of fish entirely. His chief duty was not to those men, but rather to the three helpless and vulnerable women riding in those wagons. He did not aim to have them killed or captured by the Kiowa.

When they were well into the hills

and passing through a ravine, with rocky walls towering up perhaps a hundred feet on either side, along with slopes covered in loose scree leading between the cliffs, the Major halted the wagons.

'This will make as good a spot as any,' he said, 'Unhitch those horses and then we'll make a line of the carts.'

When Archer saw what was being planned, which looked to him very much as though the soldiers were making ready for a siege, he went to the Sisters and said, 'Leave all your things here. This is life and death. Come with me right this very second and start walking up the slope there and into the hills.'

'Leave our bags, you mean?' asked Sister Agatha in bewilderment.

'Yes, do not take anything. We are climbing up there and you will not have breath to carry yourself up that slope as well as luggage.'

'May we collect it afterwards?' said Sister Theresa.

'There may not be an afterwards,' said Archer roughly. 'We must start out right this second. Come on, let's move.'

Such was the faith that Mother Veronica had placed in the young man, that the nuns now seemed to regard Archer as being their leader and protector. They set off behind him in single file. When they were clear of the wagons, which were being hauled into position by the sweating men, he heard the Major call to him, 'Archer, you mad fool! What are you about? Come back here directly!'

'Just keep walking,' he told the three Sisters, 'don't set mind to what anybody says but me.'

It was a stiff climb and the young women were gasping and panting by the time they gained the top of the slope. To their right were the rugged cliffs overlooking the road and behind them, the hills stretched away into the distance.

'We'll stop here,' said Archer. 'I want to think about this.'

Beneath them, the wagons were now arranged in a ragged semi-circle, with the open end against the rock face. They could hear faintly the shouting of the men and neighing of the horses, who were tethered beside the carts. Archer shook his head.

'That fool doesn't know what he's doing. When the shooting begins, those beasts will go wild with terror and like as not, kick somebody to death.'

'Have you been in this situation before?' asked one of the nuns.

'More than once,' he replied. 'I tell you straight, that those men down there are done for if there's more than a handful of attackers. Which, judging by that cloud of dust, I would say that there is. Hallo, what's that?' His eye had fallen upon a black opening in the rocks, a little way from where they were standing. 'You girls stay here, I want to look into this.'

Archer went scrabbling over the broken rocks and stones to where the cliff reared above them. Some freak geological process had carved a sizeable cavern in the rock face. Sizeable at least, if you were looking for some space where three women and one man might squeeze in and escape the vigilant gaze of a crew of bloodthirsty Indians. He bent down and entered the cave. It opened up a little after he got inside; the ceiling was perhaps seven feet high and the cave itself went back for fifteen to twenty feet. 'Isn't that just perfect?' Archer muttered to himself. He went back out into the evening sun and then beckoned the nuns. They trod carefully over the rough ground and came to where he was standing by the boulders, which framed the entrance to the cave.

'Right, this here's the game. You three are all going to crowd into this cave. You must expect not to leave it all night. Not for any reason in the world. Is that plain?'

Sister Agatha began to raise some objection, he did not know what and nor did he want to know. He said, 'No, this is life and death. I don't care at all for modesty or what's fitting or any of that foolishness. When the Indians come, they will kill and torture and rape. You have no idea. I do, I seen what they done to folks in the war.'

Sister Theresa was blushing crimson and seemed to be in an agony of embarrassment. 'What my Sister meant, I think — ' she began, but Archer cut her off brutally.

'Like as not, she was talking of making water or some such. That's well and good. I will stay here watching the road below. You all go and do what you must and then come back here. Don't waste a second, you hear me? When I say life and death, I mean it.'

He couldn't see the open plain from this post and neither could the Major. Archer supposed that the Kiowa or Comanche or whoever it was they had seen would be with them in fifteen minutes at the most. He resisted the temptation to turn round and holler at the girls to hurry up. They were dying of shame anyway at hearing him talk of them 'making water'. Well, he couldn't help that. There was no time for being prissy and they'd better realize that this was not in the nature of a Sunday School outing. He guessed that by nightfall, not one of those men down by the wagons would be left alive. There wasn't anything he could do about that, but he could at least save the lives of those three women.

After what seemed to Archer an eternity, the nuns returned. Without looking around again, he said, 'You mind me well. You three do not set a foot from that cave now without my say-so. I will set here and keep watch.' He loaded the Springfield, cocked it and then rested it on a nearby rock. There had been no sound of movement behind him and he turned, saying, 'What ails you now? Why have you not done as I bid you?'

'We wanted to thank you again for all that you are doing,' said Sister Theresa, 'and to tell you that we will be praying through the night.'

'That's not apt to help matters, but then again, I doubt it'll hurt. Go on now, get into that cave.'

Once they had gone, Archer picked up his rifle and sighted down it to the road below. It had been quite a climb up here and even allowing for the undeniable fact that a bunch of half-naked Indian braves would make a faster job of it than nuns wearing heavy habits, it would still take them time to get up that slope. He took out the box of cartridges, tore open the top and set it down at his side. Then he took five out and stood them up like chess pieces on the rock over which he was peering. His reasoning was simple. He hoped that the Indians wouldn't even know that he was up here, being so occupied with the men inside the improvised stockade. If, however, they did see him and wanted to kill him, why then, they would have to climb up here to do it. The boulder provided good cover, so they would need to be damned good shots to pick him off from below.

With that Springfield, he reckoned to be able to maintain a steady rate of fire at ten rounds a minute. How many of them would die, before they decided to call it a day and leave him be? While he was turning these things over in his mind, he gradually became aware of a susurration in the distance. At first it was no more than a faint rustling or rumbling noise, but then, as it grew louder, he was able to distinguish the sound of pounding hoofs. The Indians were nearly upon them.

11

There must have been at least eighty, maybe more, like ninety or a hundred riders, and at first, when they thundered around along the track and past the wagons, you might have thought that they hadn't even noticed the desperate men, crouched there with their rifles poking through the wheels of the carts. You might have thought that at first, but then, without any command being given, the riders reined in and the road was crowded with pawing horses and grim-faced men with feathers in their hair and their faces daubed with garish red and white paint.

Archer wondered what would happen next, whether perhaps the trapped soldiers would try to bargain for their lives. Then there was a cry of command, followed by a ragged volley of shots. Some of the Indians fell from their horses, which reared up in terror. Then it was sheer bedlam, with the Indians exchanging shots more or less continuously with the men sheltering behind the wagons. Most of the Indians had rifles, but at least a few must have been using bows, because at the back of the huddled mass of riders, Archer saw the flicker of fire. Then two arrows with flaming heads sailed up into the air and came down on the canvas hoods of two of the wagons. These were followed by others. The constant, withering fire from the attackers prevented anybody from being able to deal with the flames and in no time at all, half the wagons were blazing fiercely, sending up thick columns of black smoke into the twilight.

Throughout all this, Archer remained perfectly still. He knew very well that he was ideally situated to provide flanking fire and draw the attention of the Indians from the men they were surrounding. Indeed, had he done so, it is just possible that he could have persuaded the Indians that they faced a larger force than they had at first thought. Who knows, he might even have been the deciding factor in the battle and caused the attackers to run. But he did nothing at all; just squatted behind the boulder, waiting to see how long it would take the besieged men to be killed. His only concern was those nuns.

The riders had withdrawn a little, although they were still keeping up a steady fire on the men behind the wagons. More fire-arrows were launched against the position, until after fifteen minutes, every single wagon was burning. It struck Archer that if those men were really after the weapons that the army was transporting, then they were going about this in altogether the wrong way. Another hour and there would be nothing left of the powder, shot and guns.

It was not just the canvas which was ablaze now. The wooden carts themselves had taken fire and he could hear the crackling of the flames from up here, as the tinder-dry wood caught. There was only sporadic firing now from the soldiers and he guessed that most of them were wounded or dead. The Indians too had had their casualties, but there had been far more of them to begin with, so there were still seventy or so milling about. Presumably, the soldiers could no longer shelter near the wagons and were unable to take accurate aim at their enemy through the smoke and flames. What would the Indians do when they had finished with the men below? Would they think to come up here? Despite his optimism, Archer was not wholly confident of his ability to shoot dead every single one of them before they reached his hiding place.

The problem was solved in the most unexpected and spectacular fashion imaginable. It should not really have been all that unexpected, at least not to a veteran like Lew Archer. As the flames leapt ever higher, the crack of the rifle fire died away to nothing. Then it began again, with renewed vigour, or so Archer at first thought. He realized what was happening. The ammunition in one of the wagons was exploding. The Indians' ponies began jittering and jerking to one side as the cracks reached a crescendo. This was followed by a deep boom, which shook the rocks like a peel of thunder. Flaming debris flew up into the air and landed among the Indian riders. Their mounts were thrown into a frenzy of panic, which was made worse when what Archer took to be cans of oil also exploded, spraying burning liquid across the roadway.

From then on, there was pretty much a constant series of explosions, interspersed with the sharper cracks of brass cartridges going off all over the shop. Despite his strict instructions, the three sisters had crept out of their hiding place and were crouched at his side, watching the show.

'It's a regular fourth of July firework display,' he said, 'I never seen the like!'

'What about the soldiers?' asked one of the nuns.

'It's all up with them,' Archer said quietly. 'They're dead.'

Nobody said anything for a while; they just watched the burning wagons and listened to the explosions. Eventually, it all began to die down a little and Archer saw to his astonishment that the Indians were turning their ponies around and apparently getting ready to leave the area.

'I'll be damned,' he said. 'They're digging up. Maybe they think we're all dead and they certainly must know that there's nothing to be salvaged from those wagons.'

As they watched, the whole troop of riders trotted off in the same direction from which they had come. They left quite a number of their fellows lying dead by the road. It looked to Archer as though more had been killed by the explosions caused by the fire than had been shot by the soldiers.

'You ladies might get a little sleep now. I will set watch and make sure that nothing befalls you in the night.'

'What will we do in the morning?' asked Sister Theresa.

'That is what you might call an interesting point,' said Archer. 'If that little fireworks show didn't attract attention from further south, well then, I'm a Dutchman. Unless I miss my guess, somebody will be out to investigate that tomorrow.'

The nuns went back into the cave and Archer watched as the sky changed from dark blue to red and then violet. In the end, it was pitch black, with the only light provided by the stars.

He listened hard, but could hear nothing. Even the hoof beats of the Indians' horses had faded away and there was an eerie silence. From time to time, he heard from far off the howling of a wild dog or wolf and there was the occasional scrabbling of small night creatures that lived nearby. He hoped that the cave which he had borrowed was not the usual habitation of a bear or something. He hadn't smelled anything to suggest so.

In order to think more clearly, Archer rested his arms against the boulder and laid his head down on them. It was in this pose that sleep overtook him.

He awoke the next day with a guilty start, horribly aware that he had left the nuns unguarded throughout the night. He felt like a sentry who has dozed off while on duty. Not that any harm looked to have occurred as a result of his carelessness. He could smell the smoke from the still smouldering wreckage of the wagons and some injured horses were whinnying down below. He could not see his own horse and it was a grief to him to think that she had been killed yesterday; either in the gunfight or the ensuing fires and explosions.

The good Lord alone knew what the next step would be, because as far as he could gauge, they must still be at least twenty miles from the nearest Army base and town. Could the Sisters walk that distance today, without food or water? He did not see it. And that was always assuming that no Indians,

Comancheros or wild beasts descended upon them while they were making their way along the road. It was a real conundrum.

While Archer was musing along these lines, he heard a soft clearing of the throat behind him and turned to find Sister Theresa standing there. He said, 'You ladies move more soft-footed than a cat. I never hear you coming. Well. Good morning to you, Sister.'

'Good morning, Mr Archer. We are ready to follow your instructions.'

'Well now, that's heartening to hear, but I ain't precisely sure that I have any. To speak plain to you, Sister, I'm not rightly sure what the next step is to be.'

The nun gave him slight smile, no more than a momentary twitch at the corners of her mouth. 'I can't believe that, Mr Archer. The late Reverend Mother said that you were a man of infinite ingenuity.'

'Did she, by Godfrey? She was a rare one, your Reverend Mother. Still, for all that, I am plum out of ideas now.

Other, that is, than for us to start walking south.'

'I see nothing wrong with that plan. Shall I tell my Sisters to get ready?'

'Yes, you just do that. Tell you what, the walk down this slope is gentle enough, for all that it was heavy going in the other direction. Why don't I make my way down now and you and the others follow when you're ready?'

Part of this suggestion was motivated by Archer wanting to let the girls get themselves ready without his presence. He felt a little ashamed of himself for being so blunt last night. There was also the question of rooting through the debris of battle and fire, seeing if there was anything to be salvaged from the ruin. He pretty much knew the answer to that already, but there was no harm in looking. It would be a grim search, though, and he hoped to spare the sensibilities of those three young girls.

It was surely a sight easier getting down that scree slope than it had been going up. As he neared the roadway, the smell of burning became more pronounced. In addition to the wood smoke, he could now detect the sickening odour of roasted flesh; whether human or horse, he was unable to say. It was the hell of a thing to encounter before breakfast and he hoped that it would not be too much for the nuns.

As he had thought, there was little enough to be rescued from the aftermath of the battle. There were two half empty canteens of water lying by the bodies of the soldiers and that was about all that was worth taking away. The horses that had been tethered to the wagons had all been killed by the fire and there were also a few dead Indian ponies. Archer looked through the effects of the dead Indians, but there was nothing worth stealing. It was while rifling through these corpses that the nuns came upon him, having glided down the mountain as silently as they managed to move everywhere else.

'You needn't bother to look shocked,' he said. 'We will be lucky to survive the day and anything we can find that gives us an edge is not to be left behind.'

Really, though, there was nothing to be found. He allowed the girls a swig each from one of the canteens, which emptied it. He slung it to one side and then said, 'Well, there's no breakfast to be had so we had best be on our way.'

'What of these poor men?' asked one of the nuns; he didn't mark which.

'They're dead,' said Archer, 'and if we don't make tracks and set to, we're like to join them before the day is out.'

The walk through the hills was not too arduous to begin with. For one thing, the sun was not high at that time of day and they were walking in the shade. After an hour or two, Archer was aware of his belly grumbling in complaint at having nothing put in it since some time the day before. He was used to going on short commons, but did not know if the girls were. There was nothing to be done, though, so he just kept moving.

As the morning drew on and the sun

rose higher in the heavens, their stumbling along the road took on the aspect of a nightmare. They were all of them starving hungry and afflicted with a raging thirst. Some time before midday, he decided that if he didn't allow them a sip of water, then they would be fainting. There were only a few mouthfuls in the canteen and by the time they had each drunk from it, that too was empty.

'Here's the case,' said Archer, as they sat by the dusty road, 'we can either go on or sit here. I am strongly minded that one of you will be fainting if we carry on much further so I think we should just stay where we are.'

Nobody asked what they would do after that. He hardly needed to spell the matter out; they had no water and it wouldn't take long for them to collapse from dehydration. There was nothing more to be said.

They had been sitting for perhaps half an hour, when Archer was aware of a faint, trembling vibration. He could hardly allow himself to hope, but the shaking from the ground beneath him grew stronger and he was sure in his own mind that it was horses approaching. Who was riding them, that was the question.

'Off the road!' he cried and shooed the women behind some boulders a little way from the road. To die of thirst was one thing; being tortured by Indians was a far more terrible death.

The sound of the horses swelled and then they swept around the outcrop of rock around which the road bent, obscuring it from view. It was a column of bluecoated cavalry. Archer stood up and began shouting like a madman. The response was not encouraging, because an officer called out an order and two men drew carbines from holsters at the front of their saddles, cocked them and then drew down on Archer. They clearly misdoubted his purposes.

It was when the nuns stood up that the tension evaporated. Archer might have been a bandit, but a glance told anybody at once that the same was unlikely to be true of the young women in their black habits.

'We could do with water,' Archer said. 'These ladies most of all.'

'Where do you hail from?' asked the officer in charge of the troop.

'We have rode with friends of yours from the Commissary department. They are back there a ways. All dead.'

'Dead, are they by God? How so? Who killed them?'

'Indians. You will see the remains of them along the road there.'

'What became of the contents of their wagons?' asked the officer nervously.

'You mean your guns? Rest easy, the Indians didn't get them. They fired the wagons and the whole lot went up in smoke.'

'So that's what sent that signal up last night. We thought something had caught fire all right. You say that everything went up?'

'That's right. Begging your pardon, but these girls and me are just about beat. We are heading south. They are meant to be teaching school or something. I don't know the details.'

'Of course. I'm sorry.'

It was not the most comfortable arrangement and far from ideal, but the four of them rode behind troopers, hanging onto their belts. Archer wasn't too fussed, but he could see that none of the Sisters were that keen on such an inelegant and unladylike mode of travel. There was, however, nothing to be done about it.

By dusk, they had come to what was in effect a garrison town, swarming with blue uniforms. Not only were there many soldiers, but there were masses of ragged children from a camp which had been set up for those who had refuged across the river to escape the fighting in Mexico. This influx of soldiers and refugees had swollen the little village of Del Rio until it had taken on the outward appearance of a bustling town.

12

All four of them were pretty well beat by the time the soldiers deposited them in the town. Archer asked the men what this place was called and then said to the nuns, 'Does Del Rio bring anything to mind?'

'Why, yes,' said Sister Therese with a real smile, 'this is where we were all going when first we met you. It is in this town that we are to set up our school.'

'Well, I guess the first step is to find your church. There is only one that I can see hereabouts. Let's hope that it is a Catholic one.'

The church of the Blessed Virgin was indeed Catholic and the priest there had some sort of knowledge of what was planned. After he had spoken a few comforting words to the Sisters, he took Archer to one side and said, 'What are your plans?'

Misunderstanding him entirely, Archer said, 'I don't know. I might go back north after I have rested up here.'

'What are you saying?' exclaimed the priest indignantly. 'You would abandon those good women now, just when they need your aid?'

'I'm sorry, Father,' said Archer, 'but I reckon that we are talking crosswise to each other. These nuns are not my responsibility. I engaged to bring them safe to this here town so that they could start this school. I have $3,000 that I was keeping for them.' He reached into his jacket and withdrew the money, offering it to the priest.

'I don't want it,' the priest said with the greatest irascibility. 'Do you not think that I have enough to do here, without running a school as well? This is to be the project of the Sisters of Mercy.'

'Well, sir, I ain't a Sister of Mercy, nor anything like. I said I'd bring them south and so I have done.'

The priest looked at Archer strangely.

They stood like that for a minute, neither of them speaking. At length, the priest said, 'You are joined to these women. There is no more to be said on the matter. Abandon them now, just when they need you and you will be doing a shameful thing. They have more need of you now than ever. This is no time to desert your post, man.'

Casually, lest he seemed to be committing himself, Archer said, 'I might stay for a day or two, but I make no promise beyond that. Is there some building for this school?'

'Yes, there is an old barn which has been offered. It will take a lot of hard work to get it ready, though. You can use a hammer and saw, I suppose?'

'I can if there's good reason,' said Archer cautiously. He saw that the three Sisters were watching him anxiously and he smiled at them reassuringly. To the priest he said in a low voice, 'This is a scurvy trick to play on a fellow. I have already done a good deal to help and now you're trying to make me feel

232

guilty about leaving them.'

'I?' said the priest in what looked like genuine surprise. 'I am making you feel guilty? Why, man, it's nothing of the sort. It's your own conscience at work.'

He couldn't leave the girls standing there like that, thought Archer. At the very least he would have to see about finding them somewhere to stay this night and then tomorrow, he could think over what was to be done about this wretched school of theirs. One thing was certain-sure; they would not be able to get the thing organized without a bit of help. He wondered what sort of state this barn was in.

The priest was standing watching him, an inscrutable expression on his face. Archer said, 'I'll allow that I might have some type of obligation to set things up a little for those Sisters. Mind, that doesn't mean I'm a going to spend the next ten years here. I want to be clear about that.'

Then he turned and walked back to where the Sisters were waiting for him.

Archer didn't rightly know what he was going to do in the future, but for now he could see that he was saddled with these girls and this school of theirs. He hardly knew where to begin. They all looked at him with such confidence that he felt strangely cheered and encouraged.

'Come on,' he said, 'let's find you ladies somewhere to stay for tonight. Then in the morning, we'll see what's what with this school of yours.'